MIDNIGHT

ROBERT BLOCH was born in 1917 in
and Stella Loeb, both of German Jev
attended a screening of the Lon Chaney film *The Phantom of the Opera* (1925),
the scene where Chaney removes his mask terrified the young Bloch and
sparked an early interest in horror. A precocious child, he was already in
the fourth grade at age eight and obtained a pass for the adult section of the
library, where he was a voracious reader. At age ten, in 1927, Bloch discovered *Weird Tales* and became an avid fan, with H.P. Lovecraft, a frequent con-
tributor to the magazine, becoming one of his favorite writers. In 1933 Bloch
began a correspondence with Lovecraft, which would continue until the
older writer's death in 1937. Bloch's early work would be heavily influenced
by Lovecraft, and Lovecraft offered encouragement to the young writer.

Bloch's first short story was published in 1934 and would be followed by
hundreds of others, many of them published in *Weird Tales*. His first collection of tales, *The Opener of the Way* (1945) was issued by August Derleth's
Arkham House, joining an impressive list of horror writers that included
Lovecraft, Derleth, Clark Ashton Smith, and Carl Jacobi. His first novel, *The
Scarf*, would follow two years later, in 1947. He went on to publish numerous
story collections and over thirty novels, of which the most famous is *Psycho*
(1959), the basis for Alfred Hitchcock's classic film. He won the prestigious
Hugo Award (for his story "The Hell-Bound Train") as well as the Bram
Stoker Award and the World Fantasy Award. His work has been extensively
adapted for film, television, radio, and comics. He died of cancer at age 77
in 1994.

Also Available by Robert Bloch

ROBERT BLOCH

MIDNIGHT PLEASURES

With a new introduction by
BILL GILLARD

VALANCOURT BOOKS

*This book is for Michael Marcus who may not get around
to reading it for years.*

Midnight Pleasures by Robert Bloch
Originally published by Doubleday in 1987
First Valancourt Books edition 2025

Published by Valancourt Books, Richmond, Virginia
http://www.valancourtbooks.com

ISBN 978-1-960241-45-0 (trade paperback)
ISBN 978-1-960241-46-7 (trade hardcover)
Also available as an electronic book.

Set in Dante MT

Introduction

Robert Bloch (1917-1994) was born in the Chicago suburbs. He was the son of a bank clerk and a social worker, both of German and Jewish descent. Bloch's childhood was remarkably stress-free; he described it that way himself in his memoir, *Once Around the Bloch* (1993). From an early age, he read voraciously and pursued his passions both in school and at the public libraries in Milwaukee, Wisconsin, where he lived from 1927 until 1953. As a kid, he grew fond of games that involved pretend. He loved acting out scenes from stories and playing various roles for his friends. The cinema was new then, and he began to attend silent comedies and other entertainments there. He was captivated.

If Robert Bloch has an origin story, it occurred in two parts. At the Lido Theater in Maywood, Illinois, eight-year-old Bobby watched the first movie he ever saw all by himself. Knowing now where his career would take him, he could not have made a more auspicious choice. Flickering in the darkness before those sheltered eyes was Lon Chaney in the full majesty of his skeletal face and jagged teeth as he haunted the catacombs in *Phantom of the Opera* (1925). Bloch was transfixed, pinned to his seat in terror. He reported that he closed his eyes often, "opening them from time to time only to observe more horrors" (Bloch *Once* 45). He ran home and in later years quipped that he couldn't sleep for a week.

The second part of his origin story occurred a year and a half later when he and his family were taking a train trip from Chicago. His Aunt Lil took him to a newsstand with the promise of buying him something for the ride. When young Bob scooped up a magazine with a picture of a scantily dressed woman on a bed looking up in alarm at the dark-cloaked figure that emerged from the shadows, good Aunt Lil might have been surprised. She might have been frightened. She might have said no, Bobby, choose something more wholesome. Instead, she placed the quarter on the counter, and little Bobby Bloch got his first copy ever—the August 1927 issue—of *Weird Tales* magazine. His life would forever be changed.

As soon as he graduated from high school, Bloch began selling stories to professional markets, including *Weird Tales*. He began as an acolyte of H. P. Lovecraft (1890-1937), corresponding with his idol from high school through Lovecraft's unexpected death. Many of Bloch's early stories incorporated elements of Lovecraft's Cthulhu Mythos while also contributing new ideas to that shared universe. Among that writing community, whose members included Lovecraft, Bloch, August Derleth, Clark Ashton Smith, Donald Wandrei, Robert E. Howard, C. L. Moore, and Henry Kuttner, there was a shared joy in writing stories for each other and in the friendships that came from the hundreds of letters exchanged among them during the 1920s and 1930s. Some of Bloch's best-known stories of this era include "The Shambler from the Stars" (1935), "The Mannikin" (1937), and "The Creeper in the Crypt" (1937). "The Opener of the Way" (1936), a story that would contribute the title of his Arkham House collection in 1947, brought his childhood interest in Egyptology to the forefront. The common element of stories from Bloch's first decade as a professional writer is that his monsters—like Lovecraft's—came from the nonhuman world. Whether they rose from caverns hidden beneath the earth or arrived from outer space, these threats arrived to prey on a hapless and largely unknowing public.

World War II was pivotal for Bloch. During the conflict, he read voraciously about the progress of the war, especially in Europe and, even more especially, in Germany. As more and more news came out about the fate of Jews and others, he had to thoroughly reconsider his own ideas about the nature of evil:

> A casual glance at any paper will prove that the monsters currently roaming a city's streets after dark are far more horrible, in one sense, than anything Hollywood has yet dreamed up. And it was not too long ago that human beings were eliminated by the carload lots in the gas chambers of Belsen and

Dachau—certainly the pinnacle of horror as far as human history goes. (Bloch "Clown" 251)

During these years, Bloch's fiction underwent a startling transformation. He was still writing thrillers, but the focus was not on the slithering, oozing monsters from beyond. Instead, his stories tended to be about everyday people under the stress of something horrible. As he reflected in 1969, "I wanted to break away from a preoccupation with ghosts and ghouls, phantoms and funerals, coffins and cemeteries" (Bloch "Backword"). He wanted to stake out new territory, to follow his interest in psychology. As he put it:

By the mid-1940s, I had pretty well mined the vein of ordinary supernatural themes until it had become varicose. I realized, as a result of what went on during World War II and of reading the more widely disseminated work in psychology, that the real horror is not in the shadows, but in that twisted little world inside our own skulls. And that I determined to explore. (Bloch qtd. in Larson 59)

He delved deeply into the Jack the Ripper legends and wrote one of the best-known stories on the character, "Yours Truly, Jack the Ripper" (1947). This story has been adapted for radio, television, and other media dozens of times. Bloch would return to this character again and again, including in his magnum opus on the subject, *Night of the Ripper* (1984), a novel that was published just three years before *Midnight Pleasures*.

If it is not the Ripper that best represents Bloch's change from cosmic and supernatural horror toward mundane humanity's capacity for extraordinary violence, then it is likely Bloch's experience living in Weyauwega, a small town in central Wisconsin, during the 1950s, and the novel he wrote while living there. He thought he knew about small town life, how people put a premium on respectability, how important it was to be family-oriented, law-abiding, and reliable. So how could it be that in Plainfield, Wisconsin, a small town just thirty miles from Weyauwega, a serial killer could be operating, a man who had grown up there and who was known by everyone? As details of the Ed Gein case trickled into the newspapers during the final months of 1957, Bloch could feel there was a story there somehow.

A character for a new novel began to coalesce in his mind. He knew that his killer had to be somebody who was part of the community but who was also separated from it somehow. This character needed to be in regular contact with strangers, not something that's common in a small town. From these ruminations Norman Bates emerged into Bloch's imagination. Still a voracious reader, Bloch knew a bit about psychology, and he recognized that unresolved mother issues could go a long way toward providing Bates with the mental state needed to carry out his abominations. After six weeks of work, Bloch finished *Psycho* and sold it first to a publisher and then to Alfred Hitchcock. Thanks in part to the monumental success of the film, Bloch spent the next two decades writing for movies and television, including *Star Trek* and *Alfred Hitchcock Presents*, in addition to his customary, feverish output of short stories and novels.

When Bloch assembled *Midnight Pleasures* (1987), his health had begun to worsen significantly. He was beset by various ailments, each of which served to slow down his writing. Most serious were the various eye maladies that made it very difficult for him to read and write, a situation that caused him great dismay. From his teenage years onward, he was always a prolific and energetic creator, at times publishing more than one new story each month. The idea that he'd need to slow down or stop writing altogether was something that demoralized him. In *Once Around the Bloch* (1993), he lamented: "I was mindful of the fact that time was running short. Maybe there was no way to avoid dropping dead, but I didn't like the idea of doing it on page 145" (396). Reluctantly, he abandoned his work in television and film and turned his attention to what he'd like to leave behind for future readers.

By this point in his life, Bloch was keenly aware that he was not simply writing horror stories, tales of crime and punishment, or thrillers. Instead, as he considered a lifetime of work, he understood that his primary subject for all of these years was the human capacity for violence, whether it was in the form of individual cruelty or the actions of mobs. In 1985, he said: "When you really get to know people, you don't need to invent monsters" (Larson 117). Beyond the thrills and fun to be had in this amazing collection, these stories also represent the culmination of Bloch's thinking about the human tendency toward violence. The instinct for violence defines us, but Bloch never glorifies it: "I never have believed that anyone who's read *Psycho* would want to go out and become another Norman Bates" (Larson 114).

Midnight Pleasures leans toward late-career short stories, but it does contain "The Totem Pole," a *Weird Tales* nugget from 1939 that had not appeared in any of his previous collections. Another story, "Die—Nasty," makes its debut in this collection. This book was part of Bloch's plan for posterity, to put his writing into some semblance of order for future readers. In 1987, Bloch published the three-volume *The Selected Stories of Robert Bloch* that contains close to one hundred stories, none of which had appeared in the two earlier Arkham House collections. At the same time, he worked on other career-capping collections, including this one.

If you are looking for all of the stories that Bloch himself felt stood the test of time, "just about every short story I felt might bear republication" (Bloch *Once* 398), then you need to have *The Opener of the Way* (Arkham House 1945 and recently reissued by Valancourt), *Pleasant Dreams—Nightmares* (Arkham House 1960 and recently reissued by Valancourt), the three-volume *Complete Stories of Robert Bloch* (Underwood-Miller 1987), *Fear and Trembling* (Tor 1989) and this volume, *Midnight Pleasures*, which contains stories not found in any other collection. Additionally, he spent the first half of the 1940s writing about Lefty Feep, a Damon Runyan-esque ne'er-do-well whose period-specific adventures have not endured particularly well as the decades passed. His collection *Lost in Time and Space with Lefty Feep* (Creatures at Large 1987) brings back nine stories featuring that character. Together, these eight books contain 170 short stories that span Bloch's six-decade career.

In *Midnight Pleasures*, you'll meet murderous spouses, demonic (literally) psychiatrists, perhaps the world's only alien invasion / mafia story, restless and murderous spirits, and a host of other thrills, all mixed with Bloch's trademark gallows humor.

If you know Bloch's work, you already know the range and creativity he demonstrated during his long career—it's all here. If this is your first experience with his writing, welcome! There is so very much to explore.

BILL GILLARD
January 2025

BILL GILLARD teaches literature and creative writing at the University of Wisconsin Oshkosh, which is only about a half hour from Weyauwega, the small town where Robert Bloch wrote *Psycho*. His specialty is speculative fiction from the first half of the twentieth century, and he has written and lectured extensively on Bloch's career. He is the author of the literary biography, *Robert Bloch's Psycho Century*, and also writes poetry and fiction. Find out more at billgillard.com

References

Bloch, Robert. "Backword." 1969, box 247, Robert Bloch Papers, American Heritage Center, University of Wyoming.

---. "The Clown at Midnight." *Robert Bloch: Appreciations of the Master*, edited by Richard Matheson and Ricia Mainhardt, TOR, 1995, pp. 250-257.

---. *Once Around the Bloch*. Tor, 1993.

Larson, Randall D., editor. *The Robert Bloch Companion*. Starmont House, 1989.

CONTENTS

Acknowledgements

"The Rubber Room," copyright © 1980 by Robert Bloch; "The Night Before Christmas," copyright © 1986 by Robert Bloch; "Pumpkin," copyright © 1984 by TZ Publications Inc. for *Rod Serling's Twilight Zone Magazine*; "The Spoiled Wife," copyright © 1978 by Roy Torgeson for *Chrysalis 3*; "Oh Say Can You See?" copyright © 1977 by Condé Nast Publications for *Analog Yearbook*; "But First These Words," copyright © 1972 by Mercury Press for the *Magazine of Fantasy and Science Fiction*; "Picture," copyright © 1978 by Charles L. Grant for *Shadows*; "The Undead," copyright © 1984 by Robert Bloch; "Comeback," copyright © 1984 by Print & Publishing Co. for *Previews Magazine*; "Nocturne," copyright © 1985 by Charles L. Grant for *Graystone Bay*; "Pranks," copyright © 1986 by Alan Ryan for *Halloween Horrors*; "Everybody Needs a Little Love," copyright © 1984 by Robert Bloch; and "The Totem Pole," copyright © 1939 by *Weird Tales,* copyright renewed 1967 by Robert Bloch.

The Rubber Room

E mery kept telling them he wasn't crazy, but they put him in the rubber room anyway.

Sorry, fella, they said. Only temporary, we got a space problem here, overcrowded, move you to another cell in a couple hours, they said. It's better than being in the tank with all them drunks, they said. Okay, so you had your call to the lawyer but just take it easy until he gets here, they said.

And the door went clang.

So there he was, stuck way down at the end of the cell-block in this little room all by himself. They'd taken his watch and his wallet, his keys and his belt, even his shoelaces, so there was no way he could harm himself unless he bit his own wrists. But that would be crazy, and Emery wasn't crazy.

Now all he could do was wait. There wasn't anything else, no choice, no options, no way, once you were here in the rubber room.

To begin with, it was small—six paces long and six paces wide. A reasonably active man could cover the distance between the walls in one jump but he'd need a running start. Not that there was any point in trying, because he'd just bounce harmlessly off the thick padding.

The windowless walls were padded everywhere from floor to ceiling and so was the door. The padding was seamless so it couldn't be torn or pried away. Even the floor was padded, except for a ten-inch square at the far left corner which was supposed to serve as a toilet facility.

Above him a tiny light bulb burned dimly behind its mesh enclosure, safely beyond reach from the floor below. The ceiling around it was padded too, probably to deaden sound.

Restraint room, that's what they said it was, but it used to be called a padded cell. Rubber room was just popular slang. And maybe the slang wouldn't be so popular if more people were exposed to the reality.

Before he knew what he was doing, Emery found himself pacing back and forth. Six paces forward, six paces back, over and over again, like an animal in a cage.

That's what this was, actually—not a room, just a cage. And if you stayed in a cage long enough you turned into an animal. Ripping and clawing and smashing your head against the walls, howling for release.

If you weren't crazy when you came in you'd go crazy before you got out. The trick, of course, was not to stay here too long.

But how long was too long? How long would it be before the lawyer arrived?

Six paces forward, six paces back. Gray spongy padding muffled his footsteps on the floor and absorbed the light from above, leaving the walls in shadow. Shadows could drive you crazy too. So could the silence, and being alone. Alone in shadows and silence, like he'd been when they found him there in the room—the other room, the one in the house.

It was like a bad dream. Maybe that's the way it feels when you're crazy, and if so he must have been crazy when it happened.

But Emery wasn't crazy now. He was perfectly sane, completely under control. And there was nothing here that could harm him. Silence can't harm you. What was the old saying? Violence is golden. No, not *violence.* Where had that come from? Freudian slip. To hell with Freud, what did he know? Nobody knew. And if he kept silent nobody ever would. Even though they'd found him they couldn't prove anything. Not if he kept silent, let his lawyer do the talking. Silence was his friend. And the shadows were his friends too. Shadows hid everything. There had been shadows in the other room and no one could have seen clearly when they found him. You just *thought* you saw it, he'd tell them.

No, he'd forgotten: he mustn't tell them, just let the lawyer talk. What was the matter with him, *was* he going crazy here after all?

Six paces forward, six paces back. Keep walking, keep silent.

Keep away from those shadows in the corners. They were getting darker now. Darker and thicker. Something seemed to be moving there in the far corner to the right.

Emery felt the muscles tightening in his throat and he couldn't control them; he knew that in a moment he was going to scream.

Then the door opened behind him and in the light from the corridor the shadow disappeared.

It was a good thing he hadn't screamed. They would have been sure he was crazy then, and that would spoil everything.

But now that the shadow was gone Emery relaxed. By the time they took him down the hall and into the visitors' room he was quite calm again.

His lawyer waited for him there, sitting on the other side of the grille barrier, and nobody was listening.

That's what the lawyer said. Nobody's listening, you can tell me all about it.

Emery shook his head and smiled because he knew better. Violence is golden and even the walls have ears. He wanted to warn his lawyer that they were spying on him but that would sound crazy. The sane thing to do was not to mention it, just be careful and say the right things instead.

He told the lawyer what everybody knew about himself. He was a decent man, he had a steady job, paid his bills, didn't smoke or drink or get out of line. Hardworking, dependable, neat, clean, no police record, not a troublemaker. Mother was always proud of her boy and she'd be proud of him today if she were still alive. He'd always looked after her and when she died he still looked after the house, kept it up, kept himself up, just the way she'd taught him to. So what was all this fuss about?

Suppose you tell me, the lawyer said.

That was the hard part, making him understand, but Emery knew everything depended on it. So he talked very slowly, choosing his words carefully, sticking to the facts.

World War II had happened before he'd been born, but that was a fact.

Emery knew a lot of facts about World War II because he used to read library books when Mother was alive. Improve your mind, she said. Reading is better than watching all that violence on the television, she said.

So at night when he couldn't sleep he read for hours sitting up in bed in his room. People he worked with down at the shop called him a bookworm but he didn't care. There was no such thing as a bookworm, he knew that. There were worms that ate microorganisms in the soil and birds that ate worms and animals that ate birds and people who ate animals and microorganisms that ate people—like the ones that ate Mother until they killed her.

Everything—germs, plants, animals, people—kills other things to stay alive. This is a fact, a cruel fact. He could still remember the way Mother screamed.

After she died he read more. That's when he really got into history. The Greeks killed the Persians and the Romans killed the Greeks and the barbarians killed the Romans and the Christians killed the barbarians and the Moslems killed the Christians and the Hindus killed the Moslems. Blacks killed whites, whites killed Indians, Indians killed other Indians, orientals killed other orientals, Protestants killed Catholics, Catholics killed Jews, Jews killed Our Savior on the cross.

Love one another, Jesus said, and they killed him for it. If Our Savior had lived, the gospel would have spread around the world and there'd be no violence. But the Jews killed Our Lord.

That's what Emery told the lawyer, but it didn't go down. Get to the point, the lawyer said.

Emery was used to that kind of reaction. He'd heard it before when he tried to explain things to girls he met after Mother died. Mother hadn't approved of him going with girls and he used to resent it. After she was gone the fellows at work told him it would do him good. Get out of your shell, they said. So he let them set up some double dates and that's when he found out that Mother was right. The girls just laughed at him when he talked facts.

It was better to stay in his shell, like a snail. Snails know how to protect themselves in a world where everyone kills to live, and the Jews killed Our Savior.

Facts, the lawyer said. Give me some facts.

So Emery told him about World War II. That's when the real

killing began. Jewish international bankers financed the Napole-
onic wars and World War I, but these were nothing compared to
World War II. Hitler knew what the Jews were planning and he
tried to prevent it; that's why he invaded those other countries, to
get rid of the Jews, just as he did in Germany. They were plotting
a war to destroy the world, so they could take over. But no one
understood and in the end the Jew-financed armies won the war.
The Jews killed Hitler just like they killed Our Savior. History
repeats itself, and that's a fact too.

Emery explained all this very quietly, using nothing except
facts, but from the way his lawyer looked at him he could see it
was no use.

So Emery went back into his shell. But this time he took his
lawyer with him.

He told him what it was like, living alone in his house, which
was really a big shell that protected him. Too big at first, and too
empty, until Emery began to fill it up with books. Books about
World War II, because of the facts. Only the more he read the
more he realized that most of them didn't contain facts. The vic-
tors write the histories and now that the Jews had won they wrote
lies. They lied about Hitler, they lied about the Nazi Party and its
ideals.

Emery was one of the few people who could read between
the lies and see the truth. Reminders of the truth could be found
outside of books, so now he turned to them and started to col-
lect them. The trappings and the banners, the iron helmets and
the iron medals. Iron crosses were reminders too: the Jews had
destroyed Our Savior on a cross and now they were trying to
destroy the crosses themselves.

That's when he began to realize what was happening, when he
went to the antique shops where such things were sold.

There would be other people in these shops and they stared at
him. Nobody said a word but they were watching. Sometimes he
thought he could hear them whispering behind his back and he
knew for a fact that they were taking notes.

It wasn't just his imagination because pretty soon some of
the people down at work started asking him questions about
his collection—the pictures of the party leaders and the swas-

tika emblems and badges and the photographs of the little girls presenting flowers to the Fuehrer at rallies and parades. Hard to believe these little girls were now fifty-year-old women. Sometimes he thought if he met one of those women he could settle down with her and be happy; at least she'd understand because she knew the facts. Once he almost decided to run an ad in the classified section, trying to locate such a woman, but then he realized it might be dangerous. Suppose the Jews were out to get her? They'd get him too. That was a fact.

Emery's lawyer shook his head. His face, behind the grill, was taking on an expression which Emery didn't like. It was the expression people wear when they're at the zoo, peering through the bars or the wire screens at the animals.

That's when Emery decided he'd have to tell his lawyer the rest. It was a risk, but if he wanted to be believed his lawyer must know all the facts.

So he told him about the conspiracy.

All these hijackings and kidnappings going on today were part of it. And these terrorists running around with ski masks over their faces were part of the plan too.

In today's world, terror wears a ski mask.

Sometimes they called themselves Arabs, but that was just to confuse people. They were the ones behind the bombings in Northern Ireland and the assassinations in South America. The international Jewish conspiracy was in back of it all and behind every ski mask was a Jewish face.

They spread throughout the world, stirring up fear and confusion. And they were here too, plotting and scheming and spying on their enemies. Mother knew.

When he was just a little boy and did something naughty Mother used to tell him to behave. Behave yourself or the Jew man will get you, Mother said. He used to think she was just trying to frighten him but now he realized Mother was telling the truth. Like the time she caught him playing with himself and locked him in the closet. The Jew man will get you, she said. And he was all alone in the dark and he could see the Jew man coming through the walls and he screamed and she let him out just in time. Otherwise the Jew man *would* have taken him. He knew now that this was the way they got their recruits: they took other people's children and brainwashed them, brought them up to be political terrorists in countries all over the world—Italy, Ireland, Indonesia, the Middle East—so that no one would suspect the real facts. The real facts, that the Jews were responsible, getting ready for another war. And when the other nations had destroyed themselves, Israel would take over the world.

Emery was talking louder now but he didn't realize it until the lawyer told him to hold it down. What makes you think these terrorists are after you, he asked. Did you ever see one?

No, Emery told him, they're too clever for that. But they have their spies, their agents are everywhere.

The lawyer's face was getting red and Emery noticed it. He told him why it was getting so hot here in the visitors' room: their agents were at work again.

Those people who saw Emery buying the flags and swastikas and iron crosses had been planted in the stores to spy on him. And the ones down at work who teased him about his collection, they were spies too, and they knew he'd found out the truth.

The terrorists had been after him for months now, planning to kill him. They tried to run him down with their cars when he crossed the street but he got away. Two weeks ago when he turned on the television there was an explosion. It seemed like a short circuit but he knew better; they wanted to electrocute him only it didn't work. He was too smart to call a repairman because that's what they wanted: they'd send one of their assassins instead. The only people who still make house calls today are the murderers.

So for two weeks he'd managed without electricity. That's when they must have put the machines in the walls. The terrorists had machines to make things heat up and at night he could hear a humming sound in the dark. He'd searched around, tapping the walls, and he couldn't find anything, but he knew the machines were there. Sometimes it got so hot he was soaked with sweat, but he didn't try to turn down the furnace. He'd show them he could take it. And he wasn't about to go out of the house because he knew that's what they wanted. That was their plan, to force him out so they could get at him and kill him.

Emery was too smart for that. He had enough canned goods and stuff to get by and it was safer to stay put. When the phone rang he didn't answer; probably someone at the shop was calling to ask him why he didn't come to work. That's all he needed—come back to work so they could murder him on the way.

It was better to hole up right there in his bedroom with the iron crosses and the swastikas on the walls. The swastika is a very ancient symbol, a sacred symbol, and it protected him. So did the big picture of the Fuehrer. Just knowing it was there was protection enough, even in the dark. Emery couldn't sleep anymore because of the sounds in the walls; at first it had been humming, but gradually he could make out voices. He didn't understand Hebrew, and it was only gradually that he knew what they were saying. Come on out you dirty Aryan, come out and be killed.

Every night they came, like vampires, wearing ski masks to hide their faces. They came and they whispered, *come out, come out, wherever you are.* But he didn't come out.

Some history books said Hitler was crazy, and maybe that part was true. If so, Emery knew why. It was because he must have heard the voices too and known they were after him. No wonder he kept talking about the answer to the Jewish question. They were polluting the human race and he had to stop them. But they burned him in a bunker instead. They killed Our Savior. Can't you understand that?

The lawyer said he couldn't understand and maybe Emery should talk to a doctor instead. But Emery didn't want to talk to a doctor. Those Jew doctors were part of the conspiracy. What he had to say now was in the strictest confidence.

Then for Christ's sake tell me, the lawyer said.

And Emery said yes, he'd tell him. For Christ's sake, for the sake of Our Lord.

Two days ago he'd run out of canned goods. He was hungry, very hungry, and if he didn't eat he'd die. The terrorists wanted to starve him to death but he was too smart for that.

So he decided to go to the store.

He peeked through all the windows first but he couldn't see anyone in a ski mask. That didn't mean it was safe, of course, because they used ordinary people too. The only thing he could do was take a chance. And before he left he put one of the iron crosses around his neck on a chain. That would help protect him.

Then, at twilight, he went to the supermarket down the street. No sense trying to drive, because the terrorists might have planted a bomb in his car, so he walked all the way.

It felt strange being outside again and though Emery saw nothing suspicious he was shaking all over by the time he got to the store.

The supermarket had those big fluorescent lights and there were no shadows. He didn't see any of their spies or agents around either, but of course they'd be too clever to show themselves. Emery just hoped he could get back home before they made their move.

The customers in the store looked like ordinary people; the thing is, you can never be sure nowadays. Emery picked out his canned goods as fast as possible and he was glad to get through the line at the check-out counter without any trouble. The clerk gave him a funny look but maybe it was just because he hadn't shaved or changed clothes for so long. Anyway, he managed, even though his head was starting to hurt.

It was dark when he came out of the store with his bag of groceries, and there was nobody on the street. That's another thing the Jew terrorists have done—made us afraid to walk on the street alone. See what it's come to? Everyone's scared just being out at night!

That's what the little girl told him.

She was standing there on the corner of the block when he saw her—cute little thing, maybe five years old, with big brown eyes and curly hair. And she was crying, scared to death.

I'm lost, she said. I'm lost, I want my mommy.

Emery could understand that. Everybody's lost nowadays, wants someone to protect them. Only there's no protection anymore, not with those terrorists around waiting for their chance, lurking in the shadows.

And there were shadows on the street, shadows outside his house. He wanted to help but he couldn't risk standing out here talking.

So he just went on, up the porch steps, and it wasn't until he opened the front door that he realized she had followed him. Little girl crying, saying please mister, take me to my mommy.

He wanted to go in and shut the door but he knew he had to do something.

How did you get lost, he asked.

She said she was waiting in the car outside the market while Mommy shopped but when Mommy didn't come back she got out to look for her in the store and she was gone. Then she thought she saw her down the street and she ran after her only it turned out to be another lady. Now she didn't know where she was and would he please take her home?

Emery knew he couldn't do that, but she was crying again, crying loud. If they were anywhere around they'd hear her, so he told her to come in.

The house smelled funny from not being aired out and it was very hot inside. Dark too with all the electricity turned off on account of the terrorists. He tried to explain but she only cried louder because the dark frightened her.

Don't be scared, Emery said. Tell me your mommy's name and I'll phone her to come and get you.

So she told him the name—Mrs. Rubelsky, Sylvia Rubelsky—but she didn't know the address.

It was hard to hear because of the humming in the walls. He got hold of the flashlight he kept in the kitchen for emergencies and then he went into the hall to look up the name in the phone book.

There weren't any Rubelskys listed. He tried other spellings—Rubelski, Roubelsky, Rebelsky, Rabelsky—but there was nothing in the book. Are you sure, he asked.

Then she said they didn't have a phone.

That was funny; everybody has a phone. She said it didn't matter because if he just took her over to Sixth Street she could point out the house to him.

Emery wasn't about to go anywhere, let alone Sixth Street. That was a Jewish neighborhood. Come to think of it, Rubelsky was a Jewish name.

Are you Jewish, he asked her.

She stopped crying and stared at him and those big brown

eyes got wider and wider. The way she stared made his head hurt more.

What are you looking at, he said.

That thing around your neck, she told him. That iron cross. It's like Nazis wear.

What do you know about Nazis, he asked.

They killed my grandpa, she said. They killed him at Belsen. Mommy told me. Nazis are bad.

All at once it came to Emery in a flash, a flash that made his whole head throb.

She was one of *them*. They'd planted her on the street, knowing he'd let her into the house here. What did they want?

Why do you wear bad things, she said. Take it off.

Now she was reaching out toward the chain around his neck, the chain with the iron cross.

It was like that old movie he saw once long ago, the movie about the Golem. This big stone monster got loose in the Jewish ghetto, wearing the Star of David on its chest. A little girl pulled the star off and the Golem fell down dead.

That's why they sent her here, to pull off the iron cross and kill him.

No way, he said. And he slapped her, not hard, but she started to scream and he couldn't have that, so he put his hands around her neck just to stop the screaming and there was a kind of cracking sound and then—

What happened then, the lawyer asked.

I don't want to talk about it, Emery said.

But he couldn't stop, he *was* talking about it. At first, when he didn't find a pulse, he thought he'd killed her. But he hadn't squeezed that hard, so it must have happened when she touched the iron cross. That meant he'd guessed right, she was one of *them*.

But he couldn't tell anyone, he knew people would never believe that the terrorists had sent a little Jew girl here to murder him. And he couldn't let her be found like this. What to do, that was the question. The Jewish question.

Then he remembered. Hitler had the answer. He knew what to do.

It was hot here and even hotter downstairs. That's where he carried her, downstairs, where the furnace was going. The gas furnace.

Oh my God, said the lawyer. Oh my God.

And then the lawyer stood up fast and went over to the door on the other side of the grill and called the guard.

Come back here, Emery said.

But he didn't listen, he kept whispering to the guard, and then other guards came up behind Emery on his side of the grill and grabbed his arms.

He yelled at them to let him go, not to listen to that Jew lawyer, didn't they understand he must be one of *them?*

Instead of paying attention they just marched him back down the hall to the rubber room and shoved him inside.

You promised you'd put me in another cell, Emery said. I don't want to stay here. I'm not crazy.

One of the guards said easy does it, the doctor is coming to give you something so you can sleep.

And the door went clang.

Emery was back in the rubber room, but this time he didn't pace and he didn't call out. It wouldn't do any good. Now he knew how Our Savior had felt, betrayed and waiting for the crucifixion.

Emery had been betrayed too, betrayed by the Jew lawyer, and now all he could do was wait for the Jew doctor to come. Put him to sleep, the guard had said. That was how the conspiracy worked: they'd put him to sleep forever. Only he wouldn't let them, he'd stay awake, demand a fair trial.

But that was impossible. The police would tell about hearing the little girl scream and breaking into the house and finding him. They'd say he was a child molester and a murderer. And the judge would sentence him to death. He'd believe the Jews just like Pontius Pilate did, just like the Allies did when they killed Our Fuehrer.

Emery wasn't dead yet but there was no way out. No way out of the trial, no way out of the rubber room.

Or was there?

The answer came to him just like that.

He'd plead insanity.

Emery knew he wasn't crazy but he could fool them into believing it. That was no disgrace: some people thought Jesus and the Fuehrer were crazy too. All he had to do was pretend.

Yes, that was the answer. And just thinking about it made him feel better. Even if they shut him up in a rubber room like this he'd still be alive. He could walk and talk and eat and sleep and think. Think about how he'd tricked them, all those Jew terrorists who were out to get him.

Emery didn't have to be careful now. He didn't have to lie, the way he'd lied to the lawyer. He could admit the real truth.

Killing that little Jew girl wasn't an accident, he knew what he was going to do the minute he got his hands around her throat. He squeezed just as hard as he could because that's what he'd always really wanted. To squeeze the necks of those girls who laughed at him, squeeze the guys at work who wouldn't listen when he told them about his collection and yes, say it, he wanted to squeeze Mother too because she'd always squeezed him, smothered him, strangled away his life. But most of all he squeezed the Jews, the dirty kike terrorists who were out to destroy him, destroy the world.

And that's what he had done. He hadn't cracked the little girl's neck, she wasn't dead when he carried her downstairs and opened the furnace door.

What he had really done was solve the Jewish question.

He'd solved it and they couldn't touch him. He was safe now, safe from all the terrorists and evil spirits out for revenge, safe forever here in the rubber room.

The only thing he didn't like was the shadows. He remembered how they'd been before, how the one in the far corner seemed to get darker and thicker.

And now it was happening again.

Don't look at it, he told himself. You're imagining things. Only crazy people see shadows moving. Moving and coiling like a cloud, a cloud of smoke from a gas furnace.

But he had to look because it was changing now, taking on a shape. Emery could see it standing in the corner, the figure of a man. A man in a black suit, with a black face.

And it was moving forward.

Emery backed away as the figure glided toward him softly and silently across the padded floor, and he opened his mouth to scream.

But the scream wouldn't come, nothing was coming except the figure looming up before Emery as he pressed against the wall of the rubber room. He could see the black face quite clearly now—only it wasn't a face.

It was a ski mask.

The figure's arms rose and the hands splayed out and he saw little black droplets oozing from the smoky wrists as the fingers curled around his throat. Emery struck out at the ski mask, thrusting his fingers through the eyeholes, stabbing at the eyes behind them. But there was nothing under the mask, nothing at all.

It was then that Emery really went mad.

When they opened the door of the rubber room the shadow was gone. All they found was Emery and he was dead.

Apoplexy, they said. Heart failure. Better write up a medical report fast and close the case. Close the rubber room too while they were at it.

Just a coincidence of course, but people might get funny ideas if they found out. Two deaths in the same cell: Emery, and that other nut last week who bit open his own wrists, the crazy terrorist guy in the ski mask.

The Night Before Christmas

I don't know how it ends.

Maybe it ended when I heard the shot from behind the closed door to the living room—or when I ran out and found him lying there.

Perhaps the ending came after the police arrived; after the interrogation and explanation and all that lurid publicity in the media.

Possibly the real end was my own breakdown and eventual recovery—if indeed I ever fully recovered.

It could be, of course, that something like this never truly ends as long as memory remains. And I remember it all, from the very beginning.

Everything started on an autumn afternoon with Dirk Otjens, at his gallery on La Cienega. We met at the door just as he returned from lunch. Otjens was late; very probably he'd been with one of his wealthy customers and such people seem to favor late luncheons.

"Brandon!" he said. "Where've you been? I tried to get hold of you all morning."

"Sorry—an appointment—"

Dirk shook his head impatiently. "You ought to get yourself an answering service."

No sense telling him I couldn't afford one, or that my appointment had been with the unemployment office. Dirk may have known poverty himself at one time, but that was many expensive luncheons ago, and now he moved in a different milieu. The notion of a starving artist turned him off, and letting him picture me in that role was—like hiring an answering service—something I could not now afford. It had been a break for me to be taken on as one of his clients, even though nothing had happened so far.

Or had it?

"You've made a sale?" I tried to sound casual, but my heart was pounding.

"No. But I think I've got you a commission. Ever hear of Carlos Santiago?"

"Can't say that I have."

"Customer of mine. In here all the time. He saw that oil you did—you know, the one hanging in the upstairs gallery—and he wants a portrait."

"What's he like?"

Dirk shrugged. "Foreigner. Heavy accent." He spoke with all of the disdain of a naturalized American citizen. "Some kind of shipping magnate, I gather. But the money's there."

"How much?"

"I quoted him twenty-five hundred. Not top dollar, but it's a start."

Indeed it was. Even allowing for his cut, I'd still clear enough to keep me going. The roadblock had been broken, and somewhere up ahead was the enchanted realm where everybody has an answering service to take messages while they're out enjoying expensive lunches of their own. Still—

"I don't know," I said. "Maybe he's not a good subject for me. A Spanish shipping tycoon doesn't sound like my line of work. You know I'm not one of those artsy-craftsy temperamental types, but there has to be a certain chemistry between artist and sitter or it just doesn't come off."

From Dirk's scowl I could see that what I was saying didn't come off either, but it had to be stated. I am, after all, an artist. I spent nine years learning my craft here and abroad—nine long hard years of self-sacrifice and self-discovery which I didn't intend to toss away the first time somebody waved a dollar bill in my direction. If that's all I cared about, I might as well go into mass production, turning out thirty-five-dollar clowns by the gross to sell in open-air shows on supermarket lots. On the other hand—

"I'd have to see him first," I said.

"And so you shall." Dirk nodded. "You've got a three o'clock appointment at his place."

"Office?"

"No, the house. Up in Trousdale. Here, I wrote down the address for you. Now get going, and good luck."

I remember driving along Coldwater, then making a right turn onto one of those streets leading into the Trousdale Estates. I remember it very well, because the road ahead climbed steeply along the hillside and I kept wondering if the car would make the grade. The old heap had an inferiority complex and I could imagine how it felt, wheezing its way past the semicircular driveways clogged with shiny new Cadillacs, Lancias, Alfa Romeos, and the inevitable Rolls. This was a neighborhood in which the Mercedes was the household's second car. I didn't much care for it myself, but Dirk was right: the money was here.

And so was Carlos Santiago.

The car in his driveway was a Ferrari. I parked behind it, hoping no one was watching from the picture window of the sprawling two-story pseudo palazzo towering above the cypress-lined drive. The house was new and the trees were still small, but who was I to pass judgment? The money was here.

I rang the bell. Chimes susurrated softly from behind the heavy door; it opened, and a dark-haired, uniformed maid confronted me. "Yes, please?"

"Arnold Brandon. I have an appointment with Mr. Santiago."

She nodded. "This way. The *señor* waits for you."

I moved from warm afternoon sunlight into the air-conditioned chill of the shadowy hall, following the maid to the arched doorway of the living room at our left.

The room, with its high ceiling and recessed fireplace, was larger than I'd expected. And so was my host.

Carlos Santiago called himself a Spaniard; as I later learned, he'd been born in Argentina and undoubtedly there was *indio* blood in his veins. But he reminded me of a native of Crete.

The Minotaur.

Not literally, of course. Here was no hybrid, no man's body topped by the head of a bull. The graying curly hair fell over a forehead unadorned by horns, but the heavily lidded eyes, flaring nostrils, and neckless merging of huge head and barrel chest somehow suggested a mingling of the taurine and the human.

As an artist, I saw in Santiago the image of the man-bull, the bull-man, the incarnation of macho.

And I hated him at first sight.

The truth is, I've always feared such men; the big, burly, arrogant men who swagger and bluster and brawl their way through life. I do not trust their kind, for they have always been the enemies of art, the book burners, smashers of statues, contemptuous of all creation which does not spurt from their own loins. I fear them even more when they don the mask of cordiality for their own purposes.

And Carlos Santiago was cordial.

He seated me in a huge leather chair, poured drinks, inquired after my welfare, complimented the sample of my work he'd seen at the gallery. But the fear remained, and so did the image of the Minotaur. *Welcome to my labyrinth.*

I must admit the labyrinth was elaborately and expensively designed and tastefully furnished. All of which only emphasized the discordant note in the decor—the display above the fireplace mantel. The rusty, broad-bladed weapon affixed to the wall and flanked by grainy, poorly framed photographs seemed as out of place in this room as the hulking presence of my host.

He noted my stare, and his chuckle was a bovine rumble.

"I know what you are thinking, *amigo*. The oh-so-proper interior decorator was shocked when I insisted on placing those objects in such a setting. But I am a man of sentiment, and I am not ashamed.

"The machete—once it was all I possessed, except for the rags on my back. With it I sweated in the fields for three long years as a common laborer. At the end I still wore the same rags and it was still my only possession. But with the money I had saved I made my first investment—a few tiny shares in a condemned oil tanker, making its last voyage. The success of its final venture proved the beginning of my own. I spare you details; the story is in those photographs. These are the ships I came to acquire over the years, the Santiago fleet. Many of them are old and rusty now, like the machete—like myself, for that matter. But we belong together."

Santiago poured another drink. "But I bore you, Mr. Brandon. Let us speak now of the portrait."

I knew what was coming. He would tell me what and how to paint, and insist that I include his ships in the background; perhaps he intended to be shown holding the machete in his hand.

He was entitled to his pride, but I had mine. God knows I needed the money, but I wasn't going to paint the Minotaur in any setting. No sense avoiding the issue; I'd have to take the bull by the horns—

"Louise!"

Santiago turned and rose, smiling as she entered. I stared at the girl—tall, slim, tawny-haired, with flawless features dominated by hazel eyes. The room was radiant with her presence.

"Allow me to present my wife."

Both of us must have spoken, acknowledging the introduction, but I can't recall what we said. All I remember is that my mouth was dry, my words meaningless. It was Santiago's words that were important.

"You will paint her portrait," he said.

That was the beginning.

Sittings were arranged for in the den just beyond the living room; north light made afternoon sessions ideal. Three times a week I came—first to sketch, then to fill in the background. Reversing the usual procedure, I reserved work on the actual portraiture until all of the other elements were resolved and completed. I wanted her flesh tones to subtly reflect the coloration of setting and costume. Only then would I concentrate on pose and expression, capturing the essence. But how to capture the sound of the soft voice, the elusive scent of perfume, the unconscious grace of movement, the totality of her sensual impact?

I must concede that Santiago, to his credit, proved cooperative. He never intruded upon the sittings, nor inquired as to their progress. I'd stipulated that neither he nor my subject inspect the work before completion; the canvas was covered during my absence. He did not disturb me with questions, and after the second week he flew off to the Middle East on business, loading tankers for a voyage.

While he poured oil across troubled waters, Louise and I were alone.

We were, of course, on a first-name basis now. And during our sessions we talked. *She* talked, rather; I concentrated on my work. But in order to raise portraiture beyond mere representationalism the artist must come to know his subject, and so I encouraged such conversation in order to listen and learn.

Inevitably, under such circumstances, a certain confidential relationship evolves. The exchange, if tape-recorded, might very well be mistaken for words spoken in psychiatric therapy or uttered within the confines of the confessional booth.

But what Louise said was not recorded. And while I was an artist, exulting in the realization that I was working to the fullest extent of my powers, I was neither psychiatrist nor priest. I listened but did not judge.

What I heard was ordinary enough. She was not María Cayetano, Duchess of Alba, any more than I was Francisco José de Goya y Lucientes.

I'd already guessed something of her background, and my surmise proved correct. Hers was the usual story of the unusually attractive girl from a poor family. Cinderella at the high school prom, graduating at the stroke of midnight to find herself right back in the kitchen. Then the frantic effort to escape: runner-up in a beauty contest, failed fashion model, actress ambitions discouraged by the cattle calls where she found herself to be merely one of a dozen duplicates. Of course there were many who volunteered their help as agents, business managers or outright pimps; all of them expected servicing for their services. To her credit, Louise was too street-smart to comply. She still had hopes of finding her Prince. Instead, she met the Minotaur.

One night she was escorted to an affair where she could meet "important people." One of them proved to be Carlos Santiago, and before the evening ended he'd made his intentions clear.

Louise had the sense to reject the obvious, and when he attempted to force the issue she raked his face with her nails. Apparently the impression she made was more than merely physical, and next day the flowers began to arrive. Once he had progressed to earrings and bracelets, the ring was not far behind.

So Cinderella married the Minotaur, only to find life in the labyrinth not to her liking. The bull, it seemed, did a great deal of bellowing, but in truth he was merely a steer.

All this, and a great deal more, gradually came out during our sessions together. And led, of course, to the expected conclusion.

I put horns on the bull.

Justification? These things aren't a question of morality. In any case, Louise had no scruples. She'd sold herself to the highest bidder and it proved a bad bargain; I neither condemned nor condoned her. Cinderella had wanted out of the kitchen and took the obvious steps to escape. She lacked the intellectual equipment to find another route, and in our society—despite the earnest disclaimers of women's lib—Beauty usually ends up with the Beast. Sometimes it's a young Beast with nothing to offer but a state of perpetual rut; more often it's an aging Beast who provides status and security in return for occasional coupling. But even that had been denied Louise; her Beast was an old bull whose pawings and snortings she could no longer endure. Meeting me had intensified natural need; it was lust at first sight.

As for me, I soon realized that behind the flawless façade of face and form there was only a vain and greedy child. She'd created Cinderella out of costume and coiffure and cosmetics; I'd perpetuated the pretense in pigment. It was not Cinderella who writhed and panted in my arms. But knowing this, knowing the truth, didn't help me. I loved the scullery maid.

Time was short, and we didn't waste it in idle declarations or decisions about the future. Afternoons prolonged into evenings and we welcomed each night, celebrating its concealing presence.

Harsh daylight followed quickly enough. It was on December 18, just a week before Christmas, that Carlos Santiago returned. And on the following afternoon Louise and I met for a final sitting in the sunlit den.

She watched very quietly as I applied last-minute touches to the portrait: a few highlights in the burnished halo of hair, a softening of feral fire in the emerald-flecked hazel eyes.

"Almost done?" she murmured.

"Almost."

"Then it's over." Her pose remained rigid but her voice trembled.

I glanced quickly toward the doorway, my voice softening to a guarded whisper.

"Does he know?"

"Of course not."

"The maid—"

"You always left after a sitting. She never suspected that you came back after she was gone for the night."

"Then we're safe."

"Is that all you have to say?" Her voice began to rise and I gestured quickly.

"Please—lower your head just a trifle—there, that's it—"

I put down my brush and stepped back. Louise glanced up at me.

"Can I look now?"

"Yes."

She rose, moved to stand beside me. For a long moment she stared without speaking, her eyes troubled.

"What's the matter?" I said. "Don't you like it?"

"Oh, yes—it's wonderful—"

"Then why so sad?"

"Because it's finished."

"All things come to an end," I said.

"Must they?" she murmured. "Must they?"

"Mr. Brandon is right."

Carlos Santiago stood in the doorway, nodding. "It has been finished for some time now," he said.

I blinked. "How do you know?"

"It is the business of every man to know what goes on in his own house."

"You mean you looked at the portrait?" Louise frowned. "But you gave Mr. Brandon your word—"

"My apologies." Santiago smiled at me. "I could not rest until I satisfied myself as to just what you were doing."

I forced myself to return his smile. "You are satisfied now?"

"Quite." He glanced at the portrait. "A magnificent achievement. You seem to have captured my wife in her happiest mood. I wish it were within my power to bring such a smile to her face."

Was there mockery in his voice, or just the echo of my own guilt?

"The portrait can't be touched for several weeks now," I said. "The paint must dry. Then I'll varnish it and we can select the proper frame."

"Of course," said Santiago. "But first things first." He produced a check from his pocket and handed it to me. "Here you are. Paid in full."

"That's very thoughtful of you—"

"You will find me a thoughtful man." He turned as the maid entered, carrying a tray which held a brandy decanter and globular glasses.

She set it down and withdrew. Santiago poured three drinks. "As you see, I anticipated this moment." He extended glasses to Louise and myself, then raised his own. "A toast to you, Mr. Brandon. I appreciate your great talent, and your even greater wisdom."

"Wisdom?" Louise gave him a puzzled glance.

"Exactly." He nodded. "I have no schooling in art, but I do know that a project such as this can be dangerous."

"I don't understand."

"There is always the temptation to go on, to overdo. But Mr. Brandon knows when to stop. He has demonstrated, shall we say, the artistic conscience. Let us drink to his decision."

Santiago sipped his brandy. Louise took a token swallow and I followed suit. Again I wondered how much he knew.

"You do not know just what this moment means to me," he said. "To stand here in this house, with this portrait of the one I love—it is the dream of a poor boy come true."

"But you weren't always poor," Louise said. "You told me yourself that your father was a wealthy man."

"So he was." Santiago paused to drink again. "I passed my childhood in luxury; I lacked for nothing until my father died. But then my older brother inherited the *estancia* and I left home to make my own way in the world. Perhaps it is just as well, for there is much in the past which does not bear looking into. But I have heard stories." He smiled at me. "There is one in particular which may interest you," he said.

"Several years after I left, my brother's wife died in childbirth. Naturally he married again, but no one anticipated his choice. A nobody, a girl without breeding or background, but one imagines her youth and beauty enticed him."

Did his sidelong glance at Louise hold a meaning or was that just *my* imagination? Now his eyes were fixed on me again.

"Unlike his first wife, his new bride did not conceive, and it troubled him. To make certain he was not at fault, during this period he fathered several children by various serving maids at the *estancia*. But my brother did not reproach his wife for her defects; instead he summoned a physician. His examination was inconclusive, but during its course he made another discovery: my brother's wife had the symptoms of an obscure eye condition, a malady which might someday bring blindness.

"The physician advised immediate surgery, but she was afraid the operation itself could blind her. So great was this fear that she made my brother swear a solemn oath upon the Blessed Virgin that, no matter what happened, no one would be allowed to touch her eyes."

"Poor woman!" Louise repressed a shudder. "What happened?"

"Naturally, after learning of her condition, my brother abstained from the further exercise of his conjugal rights. According to the physician it was still possible she might conceive, and if so perhaps her malady might be transmitted to the child. Since my brother had no wish to bring suffering into the world he turned elsewhere for his pleasures. Never once did he complain of the inconvenience she caused him in this regard. His was the patience of a saint. One would expect her to be grateful for his thoughtfulness, but it is the nature of women to lack true understanding."

Santiago took another swallow of his drink. "To his horror, my brother discovered that his wife had taken a lover. A young boy who worked as a gardener at the *estancia*. The betrayal took place while he was away; he now spent much time in Buenos Aires, where he had business affairs and the consolation of a sympathetic and understanding mistress.

"When the scandal was reported to him he at first refused to believe, but within weeks the evidence was unmistakable. His wife was pregnant."

"He divorced her?" Louise murmured.

Santiago shrugged. "Impossible. My brother was a religious man. But there was a need to deal with the gossip, the sly winks, the laughter behind his back. His reputation, his very honor, was at stake."

I took advantage of his pause to jump in. "Let me finish the story for you," I said. "Knowing his wife's fear of blindness, he insisted on the operation and bribed the surgeon to destroy her eyesight."

Santiago shook his head. "You forget: he had sworn to the *pobrecita* that her eyes would not be touched."

"What did he do?" Louise said.

"He sewed up her eyelids." Santiago nodded. "Never once did he touch the eyes themselves. He sewed her eyelids shut with catgut and banished her to a guesthouse with a servingwoman to attend her every need."

"Horrible!" Louise whispered.

"I am sure she suffered," Santiago said. "But mercifully, not for long. One night a fire broke out in the bedroom of the guesthouse while the servingwoman was away. No one knows how it started; perhaps my brother's wife knocked over a candle. Unfortunately the door was locked and the servingwoman had the only key. A great tragedy."

I couldn't look at Louise, but I had to face him. "And her lover?" I asked.

"He ran for his life, into the jungle. It was there that my brother tracked him down with the dogs and administered a suitable punishment."

"What sort of punishment would that be?"

Santiago raised his glass. "The young man was stripped and tied to a tree. His genitals were smeared with wild honey. You have heard of the fire ants, *amigo?* They swarmed in this area—and they will devour anything which bears even the scent of honey."

Louise made a strangled sound in her throat, then turned and ran from the room.

Santiago gulped the rest of his drink. "It would seem I have upset her," he said. "This was not my intention—"

"Just what was your intention?" I met the bull-man's gaze. "Your story doesn't upset me. This is not the jungle. And you are not your brother."

Santiago smiled. "I have no brother," he said.

I drove through dusk. Lights winked on along Hollywood Boulevard from the Christmas decorations festooning lampposts and arching overhead. Glare and glow could not completely conceal the shabbiness of sleazy storefronts or blot out the shadows moving past them. Twilight beckoned those shadows from their hiding places; no holiday halted the perpetual parade of pimps and pushers, chicken hawks and hookers, winos and heads. Christmas was coming, but the blaring of tape-deck carols held little promise for such as these, and none for me.

Stonewalling it with Santiago had settled nothing. The truth was that I'd made a little token gesture of defiance, then run off to let Louise face the music.

It hadn't been a pretty tune he'd played for the two of us, and now that she was alone with him he'd be free to orchestrate his fury. Was he really suspicious? How much did he actually know? And what would he do?

For a moment I was prompted to turn and go back. But what then? Would I hold Santiago at bay with a tire iron while Louise packed her things? Suppose she didn't want to leave with me? Did I really love her enough to force the issue?

I kept to my course but the questions pursued me as I headed home.

The phone was ringing as I entered the apartment. My hand wasn't steady as I lifted the receiver and my voice wasn't steady either.

"Yes?"

"Darling, I've been trying to reach you—"

"What's the matter?"

"Nothing's the matter. He's gone."

"Gone?"

"Please—I'll tell you all about it when I see you. But hurry—" I hurried.

And after I parked my car in the empty driveway, after we'd clung to one another in the darkened hall, after we settled on the sofa before the fireplace, Louise dropped her bombshell.

"I'm getting a divorce," she said.

"Divorce—?"

"When you left he came to my room. He said he wanted to apologize for upsetting me, but that wasn't the real reason. What he really wanted to do was tell me how he'd scared you off with that story he'd made up."

"And you believed him?"

"Of course not, darling! I told him he was a liar. I told him you had nothing to be afraid of, and he had no right to humiliate me. I said I was fed up listening to his sick raving, and I was moving out. That wiped the grin off his face in a hurry. You should have seen him; he looked like he'd been hit with a club!"

I didn't say anything, because I hadn't seen him. But I was seeing Louise now. Not the ethereal Cinderella of the portrait, and not the scullery maid; this was another woman entirely: hot-eyed, harsh-voiced, implacable in her fury.

Santiago must have seen as much, and more. He blustered, he protested, but in the end he pleaded. And when he tried to embrace her, things came full circle again. Once more she raked his face with her nails, but this time in final farewell. And it was he who left, stunned and shaken, without even stopping to pack a bag.

"He actually agreed to a divorce?" I said.

Louise shrugged. "Oh, he told me he was going to fight it, but that's just talk. I warned him that if he tried to stop me in court I'd let it all hang out—the jealousy, the drinking, everything. I'd even testify about how he couldn't get it up." She laughed. "Don't worry, I know Carlos. That's one kind of publicity he'd do anything to avoid."

"Where is he now?"

"I don't know and I don't care." The hot eyes blazed, the harsh voice sounded huskily in my ear. "You're here," she whispered.

And as her mouth met mine, I felt the fury.

I left before the maid arrived in the morning, just as I'd always done, even though Louise wanted me to stay.

"Don't you understand?" I said. "If you want an uncontested divorce, you can't afford to have me here."

Dirk Otjens recommended an attorney named Bernie Prager;

she went to him and he agreed. He warned Louise not to be seen privately or in public with another man unless there was a third party present.

Louise reported to me by phone. "I don't think I can stand it, darling—not seeing you—"

"Do you still have the maid?"

"Josefina? She comes in every day, as usual."

"Then so can I. As long as she's there we have no problem. I'll just show up to put a few more finishing touches on the portrait in the afternoons."

"And in the evenings—"

"That's when we can blow the whole deal," I said. "Santiago has probably hired somebody to check on you."

"No way."

"How can you be sure?"

"Prager's nobody's fool. He's used to handling messy divorce cases and he knows it's money in his pocket if he gets a good settlement." Louise laughed. "Turns out he's got private investigators on his own payroll. So Carlos is the one being tailed."

"Where is your husband?"

"He moved into the Sepulveda Athletic Club last night, went to his office today—business as usual."

"Suppose he hired a private eye by phone?"

"The office lines and the one in his room are already bugged. I told you Prager's nobody's fool."

"Sounds like an expensive operation."

"Who cares? Darling, don't you understand? Carlos has money coming out of his ears. And we're going to squeeze out more. When this is over, I'll be set for life. We'll both be set for life." She laughed again.

I didn't share her amusement. Granted, Carlos Santiago wasn't exactly Mr. Nice. Maybe he deserved to be cuckolded, deserved to lose Louise. But was she really justified in taking him for a bundle under false pretenses?

And was I any better if I stood still for it? I thought about what would happen after the divorce settlement was made. No more painting, no more hassling for commissions. I could see myself with Louise, sharing the sweet life, the big house, big cars, travel, leisure, luxuries. And yet, as I sketched a mental portrait of my future, my artist's eye noted a shadow. The shadow of one of those pimps prowling Hollywood Boulevard.

It wasn't a pretty picture.

But when I arrived in the afternoon sunshine of Louise's living room, the shadow vanished in the glow of her gaiety.

"Wonderful news, darling!" she greeted me. "Carlos is gone."

"You already told me—"

She shook her head. "I mean really gone," she said. "Prager's people just came through with a report. He phoned in for reservations on the noon flight to New Orleans. One of his tankers is arriving there and he's going to supervise unloading operations. He won't be back until after the holidays."

"Are you absolutely sure?"

"Prager sent a man to LAX. He saw Carlos take off. And all his calls are being referred to the company office in New Orleans."

She hugged me. "Isn't it marvelous? Now we can spend Christmas together." Her eyes and voice softened. "That's what I've missed the most. A real old-fashioned Christmas, with a tree and everything."

"But didn't you and Carlos—"

Louise shook her head. "Something always came up at the last minute—like this New Orleans trip. If we hadn't split, I'd be on that plane with him right now.

"Did you ever celebrate Christmas in Kuwait? That's where we were last year, eating lamb curry with some greasy port official. Carlos promised, no more holiday business trips, this year we'd stay home and have a regular Christmas together. You see how he kept his word."

"Be reasonable," I said. "Under the circumstances what do you expect?"

"Even if this hadn't happened, it wouldn't change anything." Once again her eyes smoldered and her voice harshened. "He'd still go and drag me with him, just to show off in front of his business friends. 'Look what I've got—hot stuff, isn't she? See how I dress her, cover her with fancy jewelry?' Oh yes, nothing's too good for Carlos Santiago; he always buys the best!"

Suddenly the hot eyes brimmed and the strident voice dissolved into a soft sobbing.

I held her very close. "Come on," I said. "Fix your face and get your things."

"Where are we going?"

"Shopping. For ornaments—and the biggest damned Christmas tree in town."

If you've ever gone Christmas shopping with a child, perhaps you can understand what the next few days were like. We picked up our ornaments in the big stores along Wilshire; like Hollywood Boulevard, this street too was alive with holiday decorations and the sound of Yuletide carols. But there was nothing tawdry behind the tinsel, nothing mechanical about the music, no shadows to blur the sparkle in Louise's eyes. To her this make-believe was reality; each day she became a kid again, eager and expectant.

Nights found her eager and expectant too, but no longer a child. The contrast was exciting, and each mood held its special treasures.

All but one.

It came upon her late in the afternoon of the twenty-third, when the tree arrived. The delivery man set it up on a stand in the den and after he left we gazed at it together in the gathering twilight.

All at once she was shivering in my arms.

"What's the matter?" I murmured.

"I don't know. Something's wrong; it feels like there's someone watching us."

"Of course." I gestured towards the easel in the corner. "It's your portrait."

"No, not that." She glanced up at me. "Darling, I'm scared. Suppose Carlos comes back?"

"I phoned Prager an hour ago. He has transcripts of all your husband's calls up until noon today. Carlos phoned his secretary from New Orleans and said he'll be there through the twenty-seventh."

"Suppose he comes back without notifying the office?"

"If he does he'll be spotted; Prager's keeping the airport staked out, just in case." I kissed her. "Now stop worrying. There's no sense being paranoid—"

"Paranoid." I could feel her shivering again. "Carlos is the one who's paranoid. Remember that horrible story he told us—"

"But it was only a story. He has no brother."

"I think it's true. *He* did those things."

"That's what he wanted us to think. It was a bluff, and it didn't work. And we're not going to let him spoil our holiday."

"All right." Louise nodded, brightening. "When do we decorate the tree?"

"Christmas Eve," I said. "Tomorrow night."

It was late the following morning when I left—almost noon—and already Josefina was getting ready to depart. She had some last-minute shopping to do, she said, for her family.

And so did I.

"When will you be back?" Louise asked.

"A few hours."

"Take me with you."

"I can't; it's a surprise."

"Promise you'll hurry then, darling." Her eyes were radiant. "I can't wait to trim the tree."

"I'll make it as soon as possible."

But "soon" is a relative term and—when applied to parking and shopping on the day before Christmas—an unrealistic one.

I knew exactly what I was looking for, but it was close to closing time in the little custom jewelry place where I finally found it.

I'd never bought an engagement ring before and didn't know if Louise would approve of my choice. The stone was a marquise cut but it looked tiny and insignificant in comparison with the diamonds Santiago had given her. Still, people are always saying it's the sentiment that counts. I hoped she'd feel that way.

When I stepped out onto the street again it was already ablaze with lights and the sky above had dimmed from dusk to darkness. On the way to my car I found a phone booth and put in a call to Prager's office.

There was no answer.

I might have anticipated his office would be closed: if there'd been a party, it was over now. Perhaps I could reach him at home after I got back to the house. On the other hand, why bother? If there'd been anything to report he'd have phoned Louise immediately.

The real problem right now was fighting my way back to the parking lot, jockeying the car out into the street, and then enduring the start-stop torture of the traffic.

Celestial choirs sounded from the speaker system overhead.

> *"Silent night, holy night,*
> *All is calm, all is bright—"*

The honking of horns shattered silence with an unholy din; none of my fellow drivers were calm and I doubted if they were bright.

But eventually I battled my way onto Beverly Drive, crawling toward Coldwater Canyon. Here traffic was once again bumper-to-bumper; the hands of my watch inched to seven-thirty. I should have called Louise from that phone booth while I was at it and told her not to worry. Too late now; no public phones in this residential area. Besides, I'd be home soon.

Home.

As I edged into the turnoff which led up through the hillside, the word echoed strangely. This was my home now, or soon would be. *Our* home, that is. Our home, our cars, our money, Louise's and mine—

Nothing is yours. It's his home, his money, his wife. You're a thief. Stealing his honor, his very life—

I shook my head. *Crazy. That's the way Santiago would talk. He's the crazy one.*

I thought about the expression on the bull-man's face as he'd told me the story of his brother's betrayal and revenge. Was he really talking about himself? If so, he had to be insane.

And even if it was just a fantasy, its twisted logic only emphasized a madman's cunning. Swearing not to blind a woman by touching her eyes, and then sewing her eyelids shut—a mind capable of such invention was capable of anything.

Suddenly my foot was flooring the gas pedal; the car leaped

forward, careening around the rising curves. I wrenched at the wheel with hands streaked by sweat, hurtling up the hillside past the big homes with their outdoor decorations and the tree lights winking from the windows.

There were no lights at all in the house at the crest of the hill—but when I saw the Ferrari parked in the driveway, I knew.

I jammed to a stop behind it and ran to the front door. Louise had given me a duplicate house key and I twisted it in the lock with a shaking hand.

The door swung open on darkness. I moved down the hall toward the archway at my left.

"Louise!" I called. "Louise—where are you?"

Silence.

Or almost silence.

As I entered the living room I heard the sound of heavy breathing coming from the direction of the big chair near the fireplace.

My hand moved to the light switch.

"Don't turn it on."

The voice was slurred, but I recognized it.

"Santiago—what are you doing here?"

"Waiting for you, *amigo.*"

"But I thought—"

"That I was gone? So did Louise." A chuckle rasped through the darkness.

I took a step forward, and now I could smell the reek of liquor as the slurred whisper sounded again.

"You see, I know about the bugging of the phones and the surveillance. So when I returned this morning I took a different route, with a connecting flight from Denver. No one at the airport would be watching arrivals from that city. I meant to surprise Louise—but it was she who surprised me."

"When did you get here?" I said.

"After the maid had left. Our privacy was not interrupted."

"What did Louise tell you?"

"The truth, *amigo.* I had suspected, of course, but I could not be sure until she admitted it. No matter, for our differences are resolved."

"Where is Louise? Tell me—"

"Of course. I will be frank with you, as she was with me. She told me everything—how much she loved you, what you planned to do together, even her foolish wish to decorate the tree in the den. Her pleading would have melted a heart of stone, *amigo*. I found it impossible to resist."

"If you've harmed her—"

"I granted her wish. She is in the den now." Santiago chuckled again, his voice trailing off into a spasm of coughing.

But I was already groping my way to the door of the den, flinging it open.

The light from the tree bulbs was dim, barely enough for me to avoid stumbling over the machete on the floor. Quickly I looked up at the easel in the corner, half expecting to see the painting slashed. But Louise's portrait was untouched.

I forced myself to gaze down at the floor again, dreading what I might see, then breathed a sigh of relief. There was nothing on the floor but the machete.

Stooping, I picked it up, and now I noticed the stains on the rusty blade—the red stains slowly oozing in tiny droplets to the floor.

For a moment I fancied I could actually hear them fall, then realized they were too minute and too few to account for the steady dripping sound that came from—

It was then that Santiago must have shot himself in the other room, but it was not the sudden sound which prompted my scream.

I stared at the Christmas tree, at the twinkling lights twining gaily across its huge boughs, and at the oddly shaped ornaments draped and affixed to its spiky branches. Stared, and screamed, because the madman had told the truth. Louise was decorating the Christmas tree.

Pumpkin

Night came early in the country.

The sun disappeared into the woods and shadows started slinking out from between the trees. Twilight brought a chill wind whipping across fallen leaves and in the distance the huddling hills were hidden in autumn haze.

That's when David began moving through the farmhouse, locking the doors and windows.

It was a regular ritual now, but tonight Vera rebelled.

"For heaven's sake, must you close things up so early? We'll suffocate in here without fresh air."

David didn't answer. Instead he opened the kitchen cabinet, pulled out the vodka bottle, and poured himself a shot.

"Please, David," she said. "Couldn't you wait until after dinner? I'll have it on the table just as soon as Billy shows up."

David was staring out the window, squinting at the woods across the road, but now he turned and his eyes widened.

"I thought he was in his room," he said. "How often do I have to tell you I don't want that kid outside when it gets dark?"

"But he's just across the way—"

David turned so quickly that Vera got only a momentary glimpse of his face, but what she saw frightened her because he looked so frightened. And now he was hurrying to the door, flinging it open, rushing out.

As Vera moved to the window she could see him running across the road and into the tangled, weed-choked remnants of the vegetable garden beside the old Holloway place. Then he was swallowed up in the dusk and Vera lost sight of him.

I lost sight of him a long time ago, she told herself. *Ever since we moved here to the farmhouse.*

Perhaps it started even earlier than that, back in town, when David was terminated just before Easter.

"Terminated, hell!" he'd raged. "Bastards fired me, that's what they did. Ten years working my butt off for the company and now they're giving my job to a lousy computer!"

"It's not the end of the world," Vera said. "There must be other openings for comptrollers and you know a lot of people in the business. The thing to do is start making some calls, get out a résumé."

So David called around and circulated his résumé. He had several promising interviews, a few nibbles, and no firm offers. By Labor Day they'd run through his severance pay, and it was then that Vera suggested moving to the farm.

"You're out of your mind," he said. "I'm an accountant, not a manure spreader."

"No one expects you to work the place, darling. But it's only forty minutes from town on the turnpike and if you get a job—"

"*If*? I'll land something, just be patient."

"I am patient," Vera told him. "But we're already digging into our savings. And here you have a perfectly good piece of property your uncle left you, standing idle all these years, where we can live rent-free."

"That's crazy," David said. "The whole place is run-down; cost a fortune just to fix it up halfway decently."

Vera shook her head. "We've got our furniture and the appliances. Maybe we'll have to spend some money on minor repairs, but the house is sound. I'm sure we can manage on far less than we're paying here. Besides, it'll be good for Billy, living in the country. And it will be good for you too, getting away from this rat race."

"I don't want to go there," David told her. "And that's final."

Only it wasn't final. Vera went right ahead on her own and made all the arrangements. Their lease on the apartment was up at the end of the month and by then she'd got the painters and carpenter and the electrical contractor working against the deadline. Just as she thought, it was no big deal.

The big deal turned out to be persuading David to make the move. But she kept after him, and when it came to facing the hike in the new leasing agreement he finally saw the light.

They'd moved in at the beginning of October and even David had to admit she'd done a wonderful job transforming the old farmhouse into a comfortable home. Billy lost a few weeks of school but for an eight-year-old it wasn't important, and he liked his new surroundings—ten full acres to run wild in, plus the woods behind the abandoned Holloway place across the road.

But right from the start David put his foot down. He didn't want Billy playing anywhere near the deserted farmhouse with its caved-in roof, and he served notice that the woods were strictly off limits; in fact Billy wasn't permitted to cross the road at all.

Vera could understand about the farmhouse because it was boarded up, and there was no telling if the structure was safe. What she couldn't understand was why Billy couldn't play in the yard or the wooded area beyond.

"Private property," David said. "No trespassing. Folks out here are funny about such things."

Vera tried to reason with him. "There's nobody living within a mile of this place. And Billy isn't going to harm anything."

"That's not the point. I don't want anything to harm Billy."

"What do you mean?"

David didn't answer her. But it was then she began to notice the way he acted every night as darkness came, locking everything up. Vera believed in taking precautions—after all, you never knew who might be driving around nowadays, looking for a place to break into—but he started so early, even before twilight, and if he found anything left open by accident he blew his stack.

But it was the drinking that bothered her the most. Back in town they usually had a cocktail before dinner to help him unwind when he came home from work. Now there was no work and he wasn't sharing a martini with her; he was drinking straight vodka and going through as much as half a bottle a night. He'd gotten into the habit of sleeping in all morning and watching television all afternoon. Funny, he'd always hated soap operas before. Maybe he still did because he never commented on them, just sat staring at the tube with a sort of glazed look in his eyes. But when Billy came home on the school bus, David turned off the set and the glazed look disappeared. He watched the youngster like a hawk if he went out to play and chewed Vera out for not doing the same.

It's David I should have been looking at, not Billy. Vera frowned, peering through the window. *Where did I lose him?*

She found him now, moving forth from the deep shadows across the road and pulling Billy along by the collar. As they neared the house she could hear the muffled sounds of sobbing.

Now David's voice rose as Vera opened the door. "I warned you, remember? Why didn't you keep away from there like you were told?"

Billy raised a tear-stained face. "Honest, I was only—"

"Never mind the excuses! I give the orders here and don't you forget it. I want you to march upstairs to your room and go straight to bed."

"But, Dad—"

"You heard me. Now get going!"

Shoulders shaking with suppressed sobs, Billy made his way up the staircase as his parents stood watching in the hall, avoiding each other's gaze. The sound of his footsteps faded and they heard the bedroom door closing in the hall above.

Vera turned, speaking softly. "Really, David, must you? The poor kid hasn't even had his dinner."

"It won't hurt him to miss a meal. And he's got to learn to obey the rules. I don't want him going over there."

Vera took a deep breath. "You keep saying that, but you never give any reasons. Just as long as he keeps away from the house I don't see—"

"You don't see anything," David said. "Come on, let's eat. I'm starving."

But when she served dinner David didn't seem hungry. He scarcely touched his food; instead he got up and poured himself another drink, bringing the bottle back to the table with him.

"Want some coffee?" she said.

"No, I'm okay." He gulped the drink, then refilled his glass.

Vera took another deep breath. "You're not okay."

David shrugged. "Have it your own way. I've got no job and no prospects. Winter's coming, we're stuck out here in the middle of nowhere and God knows what happens next year when we run out of savings. Is it any wonder I'm uptight?"

"That part I can understand. But since we came here you act as if you were afraid of something—"

"Afraid? You're imagining things."

"I think you're the one who's imagining. That look you had when I said Billy was across the road tonight. And other times, when you just stare out the window."

David scowled. "I told you I never wanted to live here in the first place. It gives me the creeps."

"What does?"

He lowered his glass. It was empty, and so was the expression in his eyes. "All right. I didn't want to say anything but it's probably better than letting you think I don't have both oars in the water." He sighed and leaned back. "If you must know, this isn't the first time I've come to live here."

"David—you never told me that—"

"I never told anyone. But a long time ago, when my mother took sick after the divorce, I spent a summer and part of the fall with my aunt and uncle in this house. I was just about Billy's age then. So you see, I know."

"Know what?"

"About the place across the road. The first thing Uncle George did was warn me never to go over there, because the old man didn't like strangers."

"Who was he talking about?"

"Jed Holloway. He lived on the property all alone, ever since anyone around here could remember. Uncle George moved in here right after he and Aunt Louise were married, but he said that even then Jed Holloway was an old man. God only knows how long he'd been there or what he did to keep going. Maybe he raised enough food from his vegetable garden, because nobody ever saw him at the stores in town. Folks said he had a wife once, and after she died he never left the place, just boarded up all the windows like they are today. If salesmen or anybody else showed up he'd run them off the property with a shotgun."

"Didn't anyone ever do anything about it?"

David shrugged. "Like what? It was his place. If he wanted to cut off the water and electricity that was his own affair. He had an old well and an outhouse in back, and he must have used candles in the house because some nights you could see lights flickering from cracks between the boards on the windows. It wasn't as if he was breaking any law—just an old coot who went off his rocker when he lost his wife. Maybe he lost a kid too, because she was supposed to have died in childbirth. That would explain why he hated children so much.

"I know he hated me. Playing in the yard here, sometimes I saw him puttering around in his garden, mumbling to himself. I'd never seen anyone talking to empty air before and it scared me. The way he looked was pretty scary too—tall and skinny, with long white hair down to his shoulders and a beard that hid all of his face except the eyes. That was the worst, those eyes of his, glaring at me when he noticed I was playing outside. I'll never forget it, him standing there dressed in rags like some kind of scarecrow come to life, a scarecrow with little red-rimmed eyes staring—"

David broke off and reached for the bottle again.

"So that's why you didn't want to come here again," Vera said.

David finished pouring and raised his glass. "There are other reasons. Oh, I never believed those stories floating around about Holloway getting into magic and practicing witchcraft. That stuff about him putting curses on people and making spells to wither their crops and kill off cattle sounded pretty wild even then, and nobody ever proved anything. I probably would have gotten used to how he looked and acted if it hadn't been for Halloween."

David drank, then sat back. From the hall beyond the ticking of the grandfather's clock echoed through the silence.

Vera leaned forward. "Aren't you going to tell me what happened?"

"Jed Holloway left the house," David said. "That's what happened. Two other kids and myself, we were playing out by the barn after supper and we saw him come out and start walking into the woods behind his house. He was carrying an armful of candles and something that looked like a big book—black, with metal bands around it.

"These kids I was playing with, Tom and Terry, were older than me, and I guess they'd heard all those stories. Tom told us Holloway was going down into the woods to pray to the devil. That's what witches and wizards did on Halloween, they prayed to the devil and conjured up ghosts and demons.

"Terry didn't buy that. He said there were no such things as witches or ghosts and Jed Holloway was crazy as a bedbug. The way he acted, chasing kids and yelling at them and all, maybe it was time to teach him a lesson. So later that night, after dark, he did it."

"What did you do?"

"We tipped over Jed Holloway's outhouse."

Vera started to laugh, but David's face was grim.

"You think it's funny?"

"Of course it is!"

David nodded. "So did we, at first. I remember the way we kept giggling when we sneaked across the road. It was a moonless night, everything dark and still. Not quite everything, because far away through the trees we could see little glimmers of light. Tom said Jed Holloway must be off in the woods down there lighting his candles, and sure enough we did hear a voice that sounded like someone saying a prayer, very solemn and deep.

"That sobered us a little, that and the way the shadows seemed to move in the darkness around the outhouse up ahead. Then we set to work and forgot about being scared. The outhouse was old and rickety and quite small, but prying it loose from the foundation with a shovel was a big job for kids our age. And when we did the next problem was how to tip it over without making a racket.

"Only noise wasn't that much of a problem after all, because all at once a cold wind began to whistle through the trees. It seemed to come from somewhere back in the woods and Terri said we were in for a storm. Sure enough, the sky was pitch-black overhead and we could hear thunder growling off in the hills.

"But we didn't mind, since it drowned out the creaking when we started to lift the outhouse and tilt it over on its side. Then, just as we got ready to ease it down, lightning turned everything green and there was a clap of thunder so close and loud it almost deafened us.

"One thing for sure, it scared the hell out of Tom and Terri. They let go of their hold and took off for the road, leaving me standing there trying to balance the damned thing all by myself. I guess I was too startled to move. Then the lightning flashed again and I looked up over my shoulder.

"Jed Holloway was standing there at the edge of the woods,

and he *was* the lightning. It was playing all around his body like green fire, playing around his hair and beard and his little red pig eyes. Only it wasn't just around: the lightning seemed to be coming *from* his eyes. Then he opened his mouth and the thunder boomed right out of his throat.

"I let go of the outhouse and it dropped back into place on its foundation. At least I think it did, but I didn't wait to see. I turned and ran and the lightning followed me, stabbing into the ground at my heels. I swear one bolt came so close it grazed the hairs on my neck.

"The next thing I remember was blubbering in my bed, with Uncle George and Aunt Louise trying to calm me down. Of course they didn't believe what I told them. They even dragged me over to the bedroom window so I could look for myself. By this time the storm was howling and the rain kept coming down in buckets, but I saw that the old farmhouse was completely dark and Jed Holloway had disappeared.

"They tried to tell me he'd never been there, that it was all just my imagination, but I knew better. And when they realized I wouldn't go outside to take the school bus the next day or the day after they finally decided to pack me up and ship me back to my mother in town." David forced a smile. "So that's the way it was."

"*Was*," Vera said. "Not *is*." She met his gaze. "Look, David, I understand, really I do. Living with that traumatic experience bottled up inside you all these years must have been a terrible thing. But it's over now and you've got to realize that. You're not a kid anymore, and Jed Holloway is long dead and gone."

She rose briskly, glancing at her watch. "Look at the time! We'd better get to bed."

David's hand curled around the bottle. "I'll be up later."

Vera hesitated. "Sure you don't want me to sit with you awhile longer?"

"Of course not. I'll be all right now that I've gotten this out of my system. Thanks for being such a good psychiatrist."

"Come up soon." Vera smiled. "I may be able to offer you another kind of therapy."

Vera's smile faded quickly once she got upstairs. She'd done her best not to let David see how his story had disturbed her—not what he said, but the way he said it. Maybe telling all this would really help him; she hoped so.

Of course there was nothing to be alarmed about, but just the same she looked in on Billy before going on to the other bedroom. He was sound asleep.

That relieved her, and by the time she'd undressed and slid under the covers the tension began to ease. Now, if only David would come up . . .

The grandfather's clock tolled the hours in the hall. Windows rattled in reply, and somewhere a door groaned on rusty hinges. Vera snuggled back against her pillow, fighting a sudden childish impulse to bury her head beneath it.

No wonder David had a hang-up about returning here. To a small boy, suddenly being torn away from his home and family was a disturbing experience; living here in this lonely old house must have been an ordeal for him.

Vera sighed, shifting her head on the pillow. Thank heaven Billy didn't seem to have that problem—

"*Mommy!*"

Vera levered upright in sudden shock, alarm propelling her out of bed and into the hall.

"Mommy—"

The shrill cry rose again as she raced into Billy's room. Crouching amid the tangled covers he turned to her, eyes alive with terror. Vera sank to the side of the bed and he buried his contorted face against her breast.

"There now, it's all right." Her fingers smoothed tousled hair, soothed trembling shoulders.

"That's better," she said. "What happened?"

Billy moved back on the bed, eyes darting around the room. "Where is he?"

"Nobody's here, nobody but us. You can see for yourself."

The boy stiffened. "No, he's coming; can't you hear him?"

And she did hear something, the sound of footsteps from the hall. For a moment Vera panicked, then relaxed as David entered.

Billy looked up. "Dad—did you see him?"

"See who?"

"That man. The one who was looking at me through the window."

David strode across the room and stared out into the night. "Nobody's outside," he said. "Look—the window's locked."

"But he was here." Billy's lower lip quivered. "He was standing right there, outside."

"Now you know better than that." David turned, shaking his head. "We're upstairs here, on the second floor. So how could anyone be standing outside?"

Vera held Billy close. "It was only a bad dream," she said.

"No!" The boy pulled away. "I saw him! This old man—he had long white hair and a beard and little red eyes staring at me—"

Seeing the fear in Billy's face was all Vera could bear. Luckily for her, she couldn't see David's.

David's face was haggard in the hazy afternoon sunlight filtering through the parlor window. No wonder he was beat today; it had been a rough night before they got Billy calmed down and back to sleep again, and there'd been little enough rest for him afterward.

Vera was probably right about the nightmare; what else could it have been? She said the description of the face wasn't even a coincidence, really; most kids tend to be afraid of old men and it's only natural when they show up in their dreams.

Natural or not, David didn't want to think about explanations now because other things were more important. Bad enough that this place bugged him, but if it spooked Billy that was the last straw. He'd made up his mind this morning: they had to get out of here. Monday he'd drive back to the city and make the rounds and this time he wouldn't be so choosy, just take anything he could get, as long as they could move away before winter.

Right now the thing to do was revise his résumé, play down all that executive-experience stuff that might turn off employers who were only looking for somebody to fill an ordinary accounting job. A pay cut didn't matter; what mattered was getting out.

But it was hard to concentrate, hard to figure how to rewrite the damned thing. Maybe Vera could help; she was good with words.

David looked up and called. "Honey—can you come here for a minute?"

No answer.

"Vera—"

Still no reply, only the tick-tock of the grandfather's clock.

He pushed back his chair and rose, striding down the hall to the kitchen. He could have sworn he saw her go there, only a few minutes ago, but the room was empty now. Where had she disappeared to?

Peering across the room he saw that the kitchen door was ajar.

It was fear that forced him forward. Flinging the door wide, he moved out into the yard, calling her name. Before he realized it he was at the edge of the road.

For a moment David hesitated, glancing off into the purple haze haloing the ruined house, the weed-infested garden patch and the treetops rising darkly from the slope below. He wanted to stop but he couldn't, because he knew. It hit him the moment he saw the open kitchen door.

Crossing the road he raised his voice in a shout. No response came, and desperation drove him past the huddled house and the windswept weeds, his feet churning dead leaves as he stared at the dead limbs of the towering trees beyond.

Then he did halt, heart hammering. Something was moving down there below between the twisted tree trunks—moving and emerging.

"Vera!"

She came toward him, hair disheveled, her housedress splotched and stained. But she was smiling.

"I thought I heard you," she said.

David stared at her, numb with relief. "Are you all right?"

"Of course. Why shouldn't I be?"

"But what were you doing over here?"

She reached out and took his hand. "I'll show you."

Before he could resist she was leading him forward, down into the woods, into the forbidden forest, while the voices rose. "No—don't go—keep away from there, you hear?" His aunt's voice, and his uncle's, dead voices echoing over the years.

Now Vera's voice, here and very much alive. "After last night

I couldn't help it. Oh, I knew there was nothing to worry about, but I had to make sure. And I did find something—here."

She halted in a little clearing deep down under the trees, pointing to a cluster of matted grass and wilted wildflowers which sprouted from an oblong mound. "You know what this is?"

David blinked, silent and uncomprehending.

"Can't you guess?" Vera smiled again. "It's a grave."

She stooped, parting the tangled growth at the far end of the mound and disclosing a weathered wooden slab. It bore neither dates nor inscription, only the crudely carved lettering of a name.

Jed Holloway.

"You see?" Vera nodded toward the mound. "Now we know there's nothing to be afraid of. He's been dead and buried here for years."

Nothing to be afraid of. David nodded automatically and again she took his hand, leading him away from the dead man's grave, past the twisted trunks of the dead trees, up the path between the skeleton of the dead house and the ruined remains of the dead garden.

But the garden wasn't entirely dead. A flash of vivid color caught his eye in the rays of the setting sun and then he saw it clearly—the orange outline, rounded and resting amid the weeds. Vera saw it too.

"Look, a pumpkin!" Her smile broadened. "Just what we needed."

"Needed?" David frowned.

"Don't tell me you've forgotten. Tonight's Halloween." She stooped, reaching toward the pumpkin, but David yanked her away.

"Leave it alone."

"But, David—"

"Leave it alone, I said!"

A sudden blast of sound interrupted Vera's reply. The two of them turned, glancing toward the road at another orange object—the school bus, halting before their yard.

They crossed over to it just as Billy got out. The bus moved off, trailing a cloud of exhaust, and he turned to them, his face flushed with excitement.

"Guess what?" he cried. "We had a Halloween party at school. Miss Zelisko gave us a whole bunch of colored paper to make masks and black cats and witches and ghosts and we had a cake and orange soda and boy was it ever neat—"

"Take it easy, young man," Vera said. "If you don't slow down you'll trip over your tongue."

They moved across the yard to the back door. "You should of been there," Billy said. "All the kids, they're getting ready to go in town tonight for trick or treat. Can you drive me, Dad?"

"Sorry, son, I've got work to do." Anticipating the next question, David continued quickly. "And don't ask your mother. I'm going to need her help."

Vera glanced at him. "Maybe for just an hour, if we went early—?"

David shook his head. "I really do need you. I'm stuck in the middle of that damned résumé."

The boy's smile withered, then suddenly blossomed anew. "Okay. But I can have a jack-o'-lantern, can't I?"

"A what?"

"Don't you know about jack-o'-lanterns? Miss Zelisko made one and brought it to class for the party. It's a big pumpkin, only you carve a face on it. Then you squish out the insides and put in a candle to light up the face."

"Now I remember." David nodded. "We used to put one in the window on Halloween night when I was a kid."

"Can I do it tonight, Dad? If we put it in the front window it would look—"

"Real neat," David said. "Trouble is, we don't have a pumpkin."

"Yes we do." Billy beamed happily. "I saw one yesterday—a great big one, too. It's across the way in that old garden. We can get it right now—"

"No."

"But it's just an old pumpkin." Billy's voice took on a shrill edge. "Nobody even lives there, so it's not like stealing. Why can't I have it?"

"Because I say so, that's why." Ignoring Vera's look, David took his son's arm. "It's getting dark. Time to go inside."

Billy gazed up at him in mingled disappointment and defiance. "What's the matter, Dad—you afraid of ghosts or something?"

"There are no ghosts," Vera said.

But she wasn't talking to Billy.

Nobody was talking to Billy now. He could hear Mom and Dad in the front parlor, arguing about the resumay, whatever that was. Something you showed people when you wanted to get a job, like. Anyhow he hoped it wouldn't work because then they'd have to move back into town and he liked it here. This place was neat and even school was better than that old dump in the city. The only thing wrong was Dad, the funny way he acted lately. Like yesterday, when he caught him sneaking across the road, and tonight, not letting him have the pumpkin.

No fair, that's what it was. Other kids were going trick-or-treating, getting money and candy and good stuff like that. But he couldn't even have a plain old pumpkin lying right there on the ground across the way. What good did it do to leave it? When the frost came it would only spoil. And it would make a real neat jack-o'-lantern too, sitting there in the front window for kids to see when they came driving past with their folks on the way to trick-or-treat in town.

But what did Dad care? All he cared about was this resumay thing and now he was yelling at Mom again, real loud this time. So loud that he wouldn't even hear if somebody went out the kitchen door.

Two minutes is all it would take. Two minutes to sneak across the road and get that old pumpkin. Nobody would notice, not if you were quiet.

Just to prove it Billy came downstairs slow and careful. Sure enough, both of them were sitting in the parlor at the table under the lamp and they kept on arguing without looking up.

And the lock on the kitchen door opened easy.

It was almost dark outside now, dark and sort of chilly with a lot of clouds in the sky and a big orange moon coming up over the trees. Orange like the pumpkin across the road.

Billy crossed real fast and headed for the garden patch. He could hear the leaves scrunching under his feet and the wind

blowing through the trees down there in the woods. When he got
to the garden it was all shadows and he couldn't see the pumpkin
lying under the weeds. The wind was sort of wailing now.

But Billy wasn't afraid of the shadows. And he wasn't afraid of
that old house no matter how spooky it looked, because nobody
lived inside. If the boards creaked that was just the wind. He was
all alone here with nobody to see or stop him.

Now he saw the pumpkin next to a vine where the weeds were
hiding it. Billy bent down to reach out for it.

And felt the cold hand gripping his shoulder.

I shouldn't have scared the kid, David told himself. Sitting there
in the kitchen with only the bottle for company he stared out into
the moonlight and poured himself another drink.

How was he to know the kid would be so shook up? He'd been
shook up too when he noticed Billy was gone, and running across
the road to get him was the natural thing to do. It wasn't as if he
really feared for Billy's safety, but somebody had to teach him to
follow orders. Why couldn't Vera understand?

But she didn't understand, any more than Billy. Instead she
took his part. "Never mind that stupid old pumpkin," she told
him. "How about you and I driving into town for trick or treat?"

Stupid pumpkin. *Stupid David,* that's what she really meant,
and it hurt. Did she think he was wigging out? All he wanted was
to protect the boy, teach him a little discipline.

Instead she rewarded him for disobedience. Naturally Billy
was overjoyed and the two of them left happily together. Left
him without another word, left him alone there feeling like a
fool.

David raised his glass, watching it turn orange-gold in the
moonlight streaming in from the window. The whiskey was
orange-gold too, and as he drank it kindled a golden glow inside,
warming and expanding.

He set the glass down with a sigh. *Maybe I am a fool.* Was it the
liquor talking or did he really feel that way? He wasn't quite sure,
but now he was able to face the possibility as his anger ebbed.

Perhaps he'd overreacted. After all Billy was just a kid and his
excitement was normal for his age. It wasn't his fault David felt

the way he did about Halloween and something that had happened twenty-five years ago.

Vera was right; he was a grown man now and Jed Holloway was in his grave. Why keep him alive in his own mind?

David bought himself another drink. Bottle getting empty, he was getting full. But the whiskey was helping, helping him to think straight for the first time in months.

When you came right down to it, what did he really know about Jed Holloway? Seen through a child's eyes he'd been pure evil, but as a reasoning adult David knew nothing is completely pure or entirely evil. That talk about witchcraft was just local gossip, but even if it had been true, all it meant was that an eccentric old man got mixed up in superstitious nonsense.

There was no proof he'd ever actually harmed anyone, not even David himself. The events of that long-ago Halloween night had been colored by a child's imagination. Nothing actually happened except that Holloway had run him off his property.

Besides, he was dead now and David didn't believe in ghosts. So why was he acting this way? He'd only end up harming himself, and perhaps harming Billy too. No, Vera was right and he was wrong. No sense passing along his own foolish fears to the youngster.

Maybe it was already too late now, but at least he could try to undo the damage. He owed it to Billy, and to Vera. And there was a way.

David lurched to his feet and opened the top drawer at the side of the sink. His fingers fumbled, then closed around the handle of a big butcher knife. Pulling it out, he headed for the kitchen door. *By God, if my boy wants a jack-o'-lantern he's going to have one.*

Stumbling across the road, David felt no fear. He wasn't afraid of the night, not even when the moon hid behind a cloud. Perhaps the moon was afraid of the wind and the way the shutters banged against the boarded-up windows of the old house, but David didn't care. The woods down below were black as ink and he could hear the groaning of dead branches rubbing against the gnarled tree trunks, but that didn't scare him.

He weaved across the weedy garden, searching for the dark outline of the pumpkin on the ground below. When he found it there was nothing frightening about that either. Perhaps this was why people got the idea in the first place—carving a harmless vegetable into a hobgoblin face just to show they weren't afraid.

David knelt beside the pumpkin, wrenched it free from the rotting vine, and lifted his knife. Drink made his fingers clumsy at first, but they steadied when he went to work. Squatting in the darkness he hollowed out the inside, then sliced away at the surface. First he cut two triangles for eyes, then one for the nose below.

Now the moon came out from behind the clouds and David wielded the knife quickly, forming the mouth into a grinning gash. The result was a perfect pumpkin head and he stared at it with a smile of satisfaction.

Suddenly the face of the pumpkin disappeared in shadow, looming from behind.

Then David turned and looked up into the *other* face.

It was a wonderful surprise, seeing the face in the front window as Vera drove into the yard.

Billy saw it too and he bubbled. "Look, Mom—the jack-o'-lantern!"

Vera nodded. Gazing at the pumpkin resting against the window ledge inside she felt as though a weight had been lifted from her. The candle within the hollowed-out pumpkin danced merrily behind the eyes and nose and mouth as the jack-o'-lantern smiled its warm welcome.

Her own smile warmed as she realized what its presence meant. David had come to his senses and from now on all would be well.

She cut the lights and motor, then emerged from the car. Billy's door was already open and he slid out from the seat; he was so excited he dropped his trick-or-treat bag, and its contents spilled across the ground below.

"Pick that stuff up," she told him. "I'm going in."

The front door was unlocked and she entered quickly, not even stopping to turn on the light. The parlor was dark, but over at the window the jack-o'-lantern cast its friendly glow.

"David, where are you?" she called.

There was no answer, nor any need of one. For as she moved to the window she saw what rested beneath it.

David was slumped against the windowpane. And the jack-o'-lantern wasn't on the ledge. Instead the pumpkin was perched between David's shoulders.

On the stump where his head had been.

Somehow Vera found the strength. The strength to keep Billy in the yard while she called the state police, the strength to tell them what had happened when they came, the strength to lead them down into the woods to Jed Holloway's grave.

It had been disturbed, its surface uprooted, the earth mound yawning open so there was scarcely need to dig. But setting down a lantern at the graveside, they did. A trooper offered a sympathetic shoulder and Vera pressed against it, averting her gaze as the other two officers wielded their shovels.

One of them spoke now. "Hey, look at the coffin; the lid's all splintered."

He slid it back, then gasped.

It was his gasp that caused Vera to look up, then run forward and peer down into the grave, into the open coffin and the moldering outline of what lay within: a fully articulated skeleton, the skull mouth frozen in a ghastly grin.

Cradled in its bony arm was David's head.

The Spoiled Wife

Jerry Clayborn wasn't exactly a prince, but he knew a Sleeping Beauty when he saw one.

"I want her," he said, pointing his finger at the face behind the frost-rimmed glass.

The director frowned. "Are you sure? Remember, you have thousands to choose from."

And so there were. The block-long chamber was bordered by solid walls of glass; behind them, in three tiers of compartments measuring six feet high and two feet wide, the bodies floated.

In spite of the frosting on the glass, Jerry could still see the occupants of each compartment bobbing face forward in their freezing solutions. They came in all colors, all shapes, all sizes: male and female, young and old, ugly and attractive. The one Jerry pointed at had long red hair, exquisitely fine-boned features, and a voluptuous figure.

"That's for me," Jerry said. "Talk about your frozen assets—"

"Now, now," the director murmured. "Remember the rules. Releasing a cryogenic subject for purely sexual purposes is against regulations. Each and every one has paid handsomely for the privilege of preservation. And if and when we restore them to life, they are entitled to their full rights as citizens. They cannot be physically abused, used as slaves, or treated as mere sex objects."

"I know that," said Jerry. "I read the law."

"Then you also know the reason for these precautions," the director told him. "Cryogenic experiments date back to the late twentieth century. The problem of maintaining subjects without physical decay had been solved, but the idea that they could some day be revived, free of disease or ailments, seemed a wild dream. Then medical advances made that dream come true, and the result was a nightmare.

"Thousands of people scrimped and saved to go the cryogenic route. They were expected to be thawed out and released now that it was possible.

"But some had been frozen for sixty or seventy years; their families and friends were dead, they had no homes, no possessions. Once freed from the freezer they simply became charity cases, a burden on the economy."

Jerry Clayborn was still staring at the redhead behind the glass. He licked his lips.

"That's when the government took over," the director said. "Abolished private facilities and laid down the rules. No subject can be restored unless his or her upkeep is guaranteed by a citizen of the state."

"Sure, sure." Jerry nodded, goggling at the glass.

The director followed his gaze. "Might I ask what sort of employment you have in mind for this subject?"

Jerry smiled. "I'm going to marry her."

"Really, Mr. Clayborn—"

"What's the matter? It's legal, isn't it?"

"But not advisable." The director pursed his lips. "Experience has shown that such marriages present many difficulties. Cryogenic restorees return to life with a different value system, the product of past cultures. The longer they've been preserved the harder it is to adjust to today's standards."

The director pressed a button and a tiny spool of microfilm popped out of a slot below the compartment housing the redhaired girl. He pulled a scanner from his jacket, inserted the film, then frowned.

"The young lady's name is Robin Purvis," he said. "A very early subject dating way back to the 1970s—frozen by her family after an accidental overdose of narcotics. Of course any physical damage will be fully repaired before release."

"So what's wrong?" Jerry said.

"I told you. It's a matter of compatibility. Now if you were to select someone of more recent vintage, so to speak—"

Jerry shook his head. "I want this one."

The director shrugged. "Remember, you were warned."

"No problem." Jerry grinned. "Unless she turns out to be frigid."

★

She wasn't.

Jerry discovered that during the very first night of their honeymoon on the spacecraft. Robin Purvis was obviously glad to be alive again, grateful to the man responsible for restoring her, and eager to make the most of the situation.

During the flight she quickly adapted herself to gravitational changes and enthusiastically explored all the possibilities of free-floating fulfilment—sex in midair, sex upside down, sideways, and on the ceiling.

But after they landed and shuttled to the honeymoon suite Jerry had rented at the Aldeberan Hilton, Robin looked disappointed.

"What kind of a joint is this?" she demanded. "Where's the television?"

"Reception isn't possible here," Jerry told her. "This is a hard-rock planet."

"Super," said Robin. "Let's get with it."

So Jerry booked a guided tour, they rented insulators, and off they went. Trouble was, Robin found her outfit bulky and cumbersome, the oxygen intake and artificial-gravity unit were difficult to control, and—worst of all—the helmet mussed her hair. But she tried to be a good sport, and it wasn't until the guide conducted them to the caverns that she really blew her cool.

"Let me call your attention to these unusual geological formations," he said, through his speaker grid.

"Never mind that," Robin murmured. "Where's the hard rock you were talking about?"

"This is it," Jerry said. "These outcroppings—"

Robin glared at him through the peepholes in her helmet. "What's with you, man? Rock is to hear, not to see!"

The rest of the honeymoon wasn't much better. Robin didn't like the synthetic meals in the hotel dining room and she didn't care for the other tourists—particularly the ones from Rigel and Betelgeuse. "All those slimy tentacles," she said. "How can you stand looking at them? And eating through tubes stuck in their belly buttons or whatever—blecch!"

"Sorry, darling," Jerry said. "I thought you might find space travel an interesting experience."

"Going billions of miles just to see a bunch of creepy-looking monsters—who needs it?" Robin shook her head. "If that's your bag, all you've got to do is drop a little acid at home."

So they went home, but Jerry didn't drop any acid. He sat down on the posturpad bed in the center of the room while Robin glanced around curiously.

"No more hard drugs, remember?" he told her. "You're clean now and you're going to stay that way. Besides, there are no hallucinogens nowadays—they've all been outlawed."

"But what about that pill you make me take every night?" Robin said. "What is it, some kind of birth-control thing?"

"The director gave me a supply when we left," Jerry told her. "You must take one every twenty-four hours for your life-support level."

"So what's for kicks?" Robin surveyed the four walls of the apartment. "Living in one room is for the birds. Come to think of it, I haven't seen any birds."

"Extinct," Jerry said. "With food and oxygen rationed, we can't afford to maintain unproductive life forms."

"How about rich people; don't they have pets?"

"I'm rich enough. That's why I can afford to live on the four hundredth floor of the best condominium in town." Jerry gestured at the four walls. "We have everything we need here. Look—this wall has your dial-a-meal unit. That wall has an automatic atmosphere-recycler installation. Over there is your complete cleaning-and-disposal mechanism. And the fourth wall houses the communications system. I'll show you how they work in the morning." He patted the bed, smiling. "Right now I want to show you how *this* works."

Robin smiled. "Okay. But I kind of figured things would be, you know, different, when I came out of the fridge."

"You'll find a lot of changes, I promise you," Jerry said. "Here—before I forget—take your pill."

Early next morning Robin shook Jerry until he awakened. "Hey, man—get up!"

Jerry blinked into awareness. "What for?"

"Like don't you have to go to work?"

"I suppose so."

Jerry yawned, staggered to the wall housing the communications unit, and pressed a button. A green light flickered across its surface, then vanished.

"There." Jerry nodded. "All finished."

Robin stared at him. "You call *that* work?"

"I'm a maintainence engineer. I'm responsible for seeing that every mechanism in this condominium functions properly. Once a day I press the button. If it flashes green, then everything's in order."

"You mean it's all done by machinery?"

"Computerized servomechanisms," Jerry said. "Programmed from the control center in Washington AC/DC."

"Then you just stay home here twenty-four hours a day?"

Jerry smiled. "We can be together all the time, darling. Isn't that great?"

"Dynamite," said Robin. But she didn't smile back. And no smile came to her face as the hours passed.

Jerry showed her how to operate the dial-a-meal and order the instant breakfast which popped out of the wall on two disposable trays. It took just an instant to get rid of the leftovers in the disintegrator tube on the adjoining wall, and the apartment itself was antiseptically cleaned in less than two minutes flat.

"You see how simple it is," said Jerry. "If you want to, you can order lunch and dinner and set the timer for delivery. Then you're free for the rest of the day."

"But what are we going to *do?*"

Jerry patted the bed. "I was thinking—"

"Not now." Robin frowned. "Can't we go for a walk or something?"

"Where?"

"Outside—down below—"

Jerry shook his head. "Ground level to floor one hundred is off limits. Nothing down there but maintainence equipment."

"Couldn't I at least take a look at it?"

"Air pollution's too heavy. Dangerous."

"Don't you ever leave this room?"

"Certainly. I travel, visit friends. Like to meet a few?"

Robin nodded, so Jerry punched buttons on the communications unit until a print-out slid from a slot. "All set," he said. "My thyrox is on the roof."

The two-seater thyrox rose vertically, then sped forward, bouncing like a glass bubble between the towering high-rises below. There were hundreds of similar bubbles whizzing past on all sides and Robin stared at them, gripping Jerry's shoulder.

"Watch how you're driving!" she said. "Look out; you almost hit that one—"

"Don't worry," Jerry told her. "We can't collide. Every thyrox is on a computerized course."

But Robin closed her eyes and kept her head down; all Jerry could see was a mass of copper curls until they landed on another rooftop.

"Who we visiting?" she asked as they stepped from thyrox to airlock to interior corridor.

"Lee and Varda Thorek," Jerry said. "Nice people; you'll like them."

It proved a poor prediction. Lee and Varda were well preserved but there was still the generation gap. As Robin pointed out on the way home, what could she rap about with people who were a hundred and fifty years old?

"I'm sorry," Jerry said.

"If all your friends are like that, we might just as well stay home."

"Suits me," Jerry told her. "Let's go to bed."

Robin hesitated. "Well—if you insist—"

"I do. Here, take your pill."

The next morning Jerry punched the button and Robin dialed their meals. The cleaning apparatus whined for two minutes and then fell silent.

"Now what?" Robin asked.

Jerry pointed at a wall. "You haven't tried the communications system yet. Let me show you how it works."

"Is it like TV?"

"Better. We've got holography."

"What's that?"

"You'll see."

Robin saw. The huge wallscreen lit up and beamed forth life-sized figures in three dimensions, so natural that they seemed to be real presences in the room. Jerry switched from band to band, giving Robin a chance to enjoy each program. There was a lecture on hygronomy, a lecture on hydroponics, a lecture on hydrodynamics, and a lecture on hydraulic engineering.

"Is that all?" Robin murmured. "Where's the car chases and shoot-outs? That's what I'm into. And what about seeing something exciting—like people jumping up and down and wetting their pants when they win an electric toaster on a game show? You know, entertainment!"

"I'm afraid our programming is structured more along educational lines," Jerry said, switching off the wall system. "Still, if it's entertainment you want—" He patted the bed.

Robin nodded and undressed. But when she joined him on the bed and he reached out to embrace her, she turned away.

"Please," she whispered. "Not now. I've got a terrible headache."

"All right." Jerry sighed, then reached for the plastic container on the end table. "But before you go to sleep, take your pill."

The next morning Jerry punched his button and Robin punched hers; in a few moments they'd eaten and cleaned up the apartment.

"See how convenient the walls are?" Jerry said.

"One more day like this and I'll be climbing them," Robin told him. She paced the room. "Don't you ever do *any*thing?"

"What would you like? More space travel? I have other friends you could meet, and there's a choice of new lecture programs whenever you want. It's a full life."

"I'll tell you what it's full of," Robin said.

"If it seems dull to you, I apologize," Jerry told her. "Now why don't we just stop arguing and go back to bed?"

Robin pouted. "Is that all you ever think about?"

"But this is why I got married! My psych told me I needed an outlet."

"You tell that turkey I'm not an outlet! I'm a human being, and I'm entitled—"

"Of course you are, darling." Jerry nodded. "Just be patient. I know this is a whole new life-style, but you'll get used to it."

"Call this a life-style?" A frown furrowed Robin's face. "No uppers, no downers, no rock, no soap operas on TV, no place to go shopping or get your nails done; you don't even have any beauty parlors!"

"You don't need one," Jerry said. But now, looking at Robin closely, he realized that the flame was fading from her red hair, leaving drab streaks of mousy brown; her makeup and eye shadow had worn off to reveal the mass of freckles and splotchy blemishes beneath. And when she scowled like this she was positively ugly.

Robin's voice was ugly too, as it rose to a whining screech. "Don't tell me what I need. You and your life-style make me sick!"

"But that's just the point, darling," Jerry said. "Look on the bright side. Thanks to modern hygienic conditioning and a simple, leisurely existence, no one is ever sick. If you'll only make an effort to adjust, you can live to be two hundred."

"Another hundred and seventy-seven years of this drag?" Robin's eyes blazed. "No way!"

Jerry didn't say anything, but he thought it over. When Robin finally stopped screeching at him and flopped down on the bed, he tried to take her in his arms. She pushed him off onto the floor.

"Dirty male chauvinist pig!" she screamed.

Somehow, in all the excitement, Jerry forgot to remind her about taking a pill.

"Sorry about that," the director murmured. "I did warn you—"

"Not your fault." Jerry shook his head. "But it's quite a shock waking up in the morning with something like that next to you in your bed. Not just the puddle, but the smell—"

"That's what the pills were for," said the director. "Remember, a restoree is basically still a piece of meat that's been thawed out. Only an artificial preservative can halt the process from continuing its natural course. I'm afraid you spoiled your wife."

Jerry sighed. "What's done is done. Better luck next time."

"You mean you're going to try again?"

"Why not?"

The director rose, smiling. "Excellent." He led Jerry into the glass-walled chamber, nodding as they moved along the aisle. "I admire your perseverance. Not every man would have the courage and determination to make another such attempt. You do plan on another marriage, I take it?"

"Yes." Jerry nodded and halted at one of the frost-rimmed glass compartments as its occupant caught his eye. "Call me a romantic," he said.

The director glanced at him hesitantly. "A word of caution," he said. "This time I hope you'll benefit from your experience and make a better choice."

"Right," said Jerry, pointing. "I'll take that fellow over there."

Oh Say Can You See—

Not all yo-yos come on strings.

This one came on the end of a metal chain, linked to a pair of handcuffs.

The yo-yo's name was Arthur Hale. He'd been shot in the right hand, which was bandaged, and cuffing him to a security officer wasn't practical.

At least that's what Dr. Osgood told me. "You understand the problem, Chief. Cuff his right hand to the security officer's left and every movement would cause him severe pain."

"That's nothing compared to the pain you're causing me," I said. "Why didn't you cuff his left hand to the security officer's right?"

"Because the officer is right-handed."

"You couldn't find a left-handed security officer?"

Dr. Osgood bit his lip. "Sorry, there wasn't time to check. You seemed to be in such a hurry—"

"No matter." Truth to tell, sometimes I think they're all yo-yos, Dr. Osgood included. But I wasn't about to quibble; the main thing was that Arthur Hale was here in my office.

I glanced at the security officer holding the end of the chain attached to the handcuffs. "Let go," I said.

He frowned. "But, Chief—"

"Let him go."

He released the chain and Arthur Hale gave me a grateful smile.

"Sit down, Mr. Hale."

"Thank you."

"Now then, Mr. Hale. I understand you have something to tell me."

Hale nodded quickly, then hesitated, eyeing the officer standing beside him.

I got the message. "Officer, you can wait outside."

"But, Chief—"

"Outside," I said. "This is no place for a man with a limited vocabulary."

The officer went out, closing the door behind him.

I smiled at Arthur Hale. "Okay?"

He looked at Dr. Osgood, but I shook my head. "Doc stays. Anything you have to say to me can be said to him. Besides, if it's as important as you claim, a witness might be helpful."

Hale didn't say anything.

"Don't be difficult," I said. "We've already made every concession you insisted on. You wanted to talk to the top man in the Bureau, and that's what you're doing. You stipulated there'd be no transcript, no taping, no bugging, and I agreed. Go ahead, check out the room if you like."

"I'll take your word for it."

"Good." I leaned back and smiled at him. "You can trust Doc and you can trust me. And if your information is as valuable as you say it is, maybe we can work out a state's-evidence deal. After all, in matters like these, there's a precedent for granting immunity to citizens—"

"I'm not a citizen," said Arthur Hale. "I'm an alien."

"Illegal alien, eh?"

"Not illegal, either. Just an alien."

I looked at Dr. Osgood and he nodded. "What did I tell you?"

"Never mind what you told me," I said. "I want to hear it from him."

Arthur Hale sat there, a plump little man with brown hair, fair complexion, and all the usual appendages—two arms, two legs, and only one head. It didn't even rattle when he shook it.

"I come from Vespix," he said.

"Never heard of it."

"Near Cygo, only a few million light-years away from—"

"Spare me the geography lesson."

"We have been observing your planet for some time, of course, from our transmittal craft. Once our *hetchors* completed their observations and gathered sufficient data, they decided on a policy of infiltration. It was then that they hatched me."

"Hatched?"

"Figure of speech. There's no exact word for the process in any of your languages. The first step combined artificial insemination with—"

"No biology lessons, either. Get on with it. Your people decided to take over?"

"Infiltrate," said Arthur Hale. "That's what I was conditioned for. Endless *fizors* of study and training, until I was ready for my mission. Our *ptyra* is a perfectionist, and once I satisfied him I knew I could pass for human anywhere." He smiled at Dr. Osgood. "I fooled you, didn't I?"

"You didn't fool anybody," said Osgood. "We've got the lab tests, X rays, EEGs, EKGs, the works. You're human, all right."

Arthur Hale shrugged. "What about the invisibility?" he said.

Dr. Osgood frowned at me. "You see? That's the other delusion I told you about—"

"Never mind," I said. I nodded at the little man with the bandaged hand. "So your people made you invisible, eh?"

"Not *made* me. They perfected a method I could use. It's a technical thing, involving optical occlusion."

"Something he saw on a television show," Dr. Osgood muttered. "That's where a lot of them get their ideas from. Once it was witchcraft legends. Now it's TV, the new mythology—"

"It's not like that at all," Hale told me. "There's no mechanical device, no so-called force field, and no time limitation. All I do is *will* myself to vanish."

"Then why didn't you vanish when they caught you?" Osgood snapped.

"Because I was unconscious. The bullet wound in my hand—"

"And afterward, in the hospital?"

"I don't know. You injected me with something that disturbed the body-chemistry balance."

"Antibiotics."

"Whatever it is, as long as it's in my system, I can't function."

"You're functioning, all right! Making a big stink about seeing the chief, handing out that hype about a matter of life and death—"

"Shut up!" I said. "Shut up and let him talk." I gestured at

Arthur Hale. "Let's begin at the beginning. Your people sent you here to infiltrate. That's a polite term for an espionage assignment, isn't it?"

"Correct. A spying mission."

"They equipped you with the power of rendering yourself invisible as a protection and set you down on earth. You'd been programmed to learn the language and customs, your frame of reference had been tested, your cover was foolproof."

"Exactly." Hale nodded. "It had to be that way if I expected to survive. There could be no margin of error if I was to make a firsthand study of the rulers of this planet."

"You knew who these rulers were?"

"Naturally. We have monitored your society quite thoroughly. I was set down at a spot where I could make immediate contact with the top leadership."

"Where was this? Washington—Moscow—Peking?"

"Ramapo Mountains."

"Never heard of the town."

"It's not a town. Just a place in New Jersey."

I frowned. "But what does some godforsaken spot in the mountains of New Jersey have to do with the rulers of this planet?"

"Everything," said Arthur Hale. "That happens to be Mafia headquarters."

I listened to Arthur Hale's story without comment and that's the way I will report it here.

Just how long the Vespixians had been observing earth or by what exact means, he did not say. Perhaps their arrival touched off the so-called flying saucer scare following WWII. According to him, their probing and scanning devices were highly sophisticated—some sort of advanced computer hardware that picked up, interpreted, correlated and stored data on a worldwide scale. Since their avowed purpose was to eventually establish contact with the highest authorities, they studied their findings accordingly.

At first, Hale said, the answer seemed obvious. Since the world is divided into nations, the heads of state controlled it.

Upon examination, however, the heads of state did not appear to be superior specimens of humanity. A Teutonic madman, a Slavic thug, a Latin megalomaniac, a Chinese warlord, Japanese fanatics and an opposing array of egomaniacal chauvinists hardly qualified as top intellects, and their political mistakes had led to a global holocaust. Still, the war had been waged at their command, a war in which millions had perished. And then—again at their command—peace was finally proclaimed. Surely this demonstration of power showed their supremacy.

Not so, said the data. War had been declared only when the national leaders were confident of their weaponry. And peace had come only when that weaponry was overshadowed by a still greater weapon—the so-called atomic bomb.

The real rulers of the world must therefore be those controlling the weapons—the military establishment.

So military minds were studied. And the generals and admirals, the tactical geniuses and masters of strategy, were judged according to their deeds and decisions. What emerged was a record of blunders and confusion which resulted in wholesale massacre; errors which led entire armies to their doom; confusion and stubborn refusal to face facts, arrogant ignorance and blind determination that ended in utter chaos. Surprise attacks and ill-planned invasions had not won a war, nor had the generals who ordered them.

Perhaps control of weaponry was not the answer. The real rulers were those who devised those weapons—the scientists, the inventors.

But further research disclosed a fallacy. If science was the seat of power, then why were scientists so powerless? Why did they labor so obediently in the cause of destruction; why were the so-called greatest intellects willing to devote themselves to the concoction of napalm, nerve gas, bigger aircraft to carry bigger bombs, and all the other devices of destruction? Even in peace, their rocketry and spacecraft came under governmental control, and so did their major experimental projects, including medical research.

No, it was not the scientists who ruled, nor the academicians— for educators also functioned under close restrictions, teaching only those truths which were self-evident to the best interests of those in power.

Who, then, was in power?

Again the Vespixians consulted their findings. And came, inevitably, to the consideration of religion. All through the ages men had fought and died for their beliefs, sacrificing themselves gladly for a thousand different gods. But none of the gods had prevailed, and those who commanded the sacrifices were singularly and significantly quite powerless to stop secular warfare. And when a scan of recorded history reached the point where Napoleon impatiently snatched the imperial diadem from the Pope and crowned himself with his own hands, the Vespixians regretfully eliminated another possible power source.

What then was left? Mankind's existence depended on his food supply, and food was controlled by agriculture. But agriculture depended on industry to implement production, and industry depended on commerce for distribution of its goods, and commerce depended on monetary exchange and monetary exchange depended upon banking and financial institutions. Money makes the world go round; perhaps that was the answer!

The trouble was that banks operated under governmental controls, and government was itself controlled by politicians and politicians were controlled by pressure groups, lobbies, labor unions, and other forces representing special interests of the population. All of these factions seemed to employ the same methods to achieve their ends: public relations and propaganda.

Which led inevitably, as the Vespixian theorists discovered, to the mass media. Newspapers, magazines, motion pictures, radio, television—these were the real makers and shakers, the powers in the land.

For one glorious moment, they thought they had found the answer: the real rulers of the world were Walter Cronkite and Johnny Carson. Until further research disclosed that most of the moving and shaking was just waste motion. The great religious books had not reformed mankind, the ethnic problem had not been solved by Harriet Beecher Stowe, and Karl Marx's ideology had nowhere been put into actual practice by the nations professing to embrace it. Theater and film offered a choice of sensationalism or inanity. Radio and the visual media pimped for whatever products paid the bills, catering to the taste of the masses or the growing lack of taste of the self-proclaimed intelligentsia. Shortly after hearing their first singing commercial, the Vespixian research team turned off and dropped out.

Humanity, they concluded, was a far more complex condition than they had thought. A survey of its strengths had failed to disclose the source of the power which controlled it.

But what about its weaknesses?

Some humans strove for virtue, and a few actually achieved it. But the majority were addicted to vice. Lying, cheating, and stealing seemed obvious enough; not so obvious was the fact that these were mechanisms, mere means to an end. And the end was the gratification of impulse.

In every stratum of every culture the common denominator was a desire for self-indulgence. The indiscriminate satisfaction of prohibited forms of sexual activity, a preoccupation with violence and brutality rationalized and ritualized as spectator sports, a mania for gambling, an addiction to alcohol and hallucinogenic drugs.

And in every society there was a so-called criminal element which catered to such needs and controlled their supply.

This control, the Vespixians realized, was the supreme source of power.

At one time such power rested in many hands; at first individuals, then small groups or gangs. But then the gangs united in larger alliances—and under the pressures of modern technology, the national criminal leaders combined forces with one another to form an international organization.

"And that," Arthur Hale said, "is how we finally discovered the Mafia."

"But that's not exactly a secret." Dr. Osgood frowned. "Everybody knows about the Cosa Nostra. They've been publicized, investigated by the government. And they're not all that powerful; plenty of their top men have been put away—"

"We found that out too." Hale stirred in his seat, rattling the chain which dangled from his cuffed wrists. "But what interested us is a point which everyone seems to overlook. In spite of the

publicity, the Mafia continued to flourish. In spite of the inves-
tigations, the Mafia kept on expanding, moving into so-called
respectable businesses, taking over control of management
through dummy corporations and workers through secret dom-
ination of unions, even combining forces with high-level governmental agencies for various illicit activities. As for the so-called
top men that have been convicted and imprisoned—are you sure
this isn't just what your slang designates as window dressing?
Because the organization is still growing. Now it has learned
to hide beneath the cloak of respectability—and no one really
knows just how far it has penetrated into legitimate enterprise
and established government everywhere. Our findings pointed
to an obvious conclusion: the supposedly top leaders are front
men, figureheads. Somewhere behind them is a supreme force,
and he's the one with the power.

"My mission was to infiltrate the organization and find the
leader."

I stared at Arthur Hale. "Don't lie to me," I said. "Your people
found him for you. That's why you were set down in the Ramapo
Mountains, equipped with the power of invisibility.

"Your real mission was to kill him."

Finding the man had not been easy, Hale said. It was like
searching for a needle in a haystack—a haystack of history dating
back to 1262, when the first *mafiosi* banded together as an underground political organization against tyrannical rule in Palermo.
Sicilian governments rose and fell, but the Mafia remained, growing in secret strength.

In 1889 it surfaced in this country, in New Orleans, as a small
group specializing in terrorism and extortion. Vigilante activity
disposed of some of its members, but others survived to prey on
Italian immigrants pouring into the metropolitan centers of the
nation.

The Vespixians researched its growth and pinpointed its
changeover from a purely Sicilian operation to an international
crime syndicate with members from every ethnic group and
every level of society—and its secret takeover of society as a
whole.

The transition was a staggering phenomenon, but what they finally zeroed in on was the constant element.

One thing had never changed, and that was the Mafia hierarchy, the Mafia tradition.

The pyramidal structure had a broad base. At the bottom were the allies, the owners of small businesses, the seemingly respectable citizens who fronted for those above and paid them tribute.

Next came the petty criminals—the "juice men," as the loan sharks were called; the smugglers, go-betweens, pimps, pushers, thieves, bookmakers, and gamblers.

They in turn were protected by a higher echelon of "muscle" which enforced their extortions and quieted complaints.

Above them were the hit men, the specialists in murder who took over the "contracts" to kill.

Once they had been numbered among the "soldiers" or "button men"—the general middle-class membership. But in recent years such members had actually become middle-class, venturing into real estate, entertainment, hotel management, financial corporations, and large-scale retail merchandising, positions of control in the fields of labor relations and management.

Their leadership consisted of families, each headed by a *caporegime* and advised by a *consigliere* who issued the orders.

But the source of those orders was the apex of the pyramid—the supreme ruler, the Don.

"This much we knew," Arthur Hale said. "And nothing more. The identity of the Don was the insoluble mystery. No matter how thoroughly we checked and hunted, we simply couldn't locate him. Our search led us to the top of the pyramid, but the figure enthroned upon it was lost in an impenetrable cloud."

"Then how did you find him?" I said.

"I told you there were two things that never changed—the Mafia hierarchy and the Mafia tradition. Tracing the hierarchy brought us to our man. But it was by tracing the tradition that we finally identified him.

"The mafiosi live by an ancient code, a way of life riddled with ritual. The most modern method of killing a traitor or informer is still preceded by the customary kiss of death. Orders are transmitted in time-honored terms. Even today the cry of revenge remains—*Livarsi na petra di la scarpa!*—meaning, 'Take the stone out of my shoe!' And part of that grand tradition is ceremony and protocol, the deference and courtesy shown to one's superiors. The greatest homage, of course, is paid to the Don.

"Monitoring the movements of the *capiregime,* we discovered a common phenomenon. Once or twice a year the head of every family made a trip to New Jersey, to a little motel in the Ramapo Mountain area. Obviously this was a summit meeting, and obviously the Don would be present. And when we learned that such a gathering was scheduled for last Sunday, I was sent down to attend it."

"Invisibly?"

"Of course. How else would I be able to move undetected, to see and hear—"

"And to kill."

Arthur Hale shrugged. "To destroy the serpent, one must first cut off its head."

"Another mafioso saying?"

"Vespixian."

Dr. Osgood gave me one of those *how-long-are-you-going-to-humor-this-weirdo* looks, but I ignored him.

"Tell me what happened," I said.

They set him down, Arthur Hale told me, shortly before dawn.

For a moment the Vespixian vessel hovered overhead, then disappeared into the stratosphere. Hale was left alone, shivering in the early morning mist, as he crouched in the bushes across the road from the Sunny View Motel.

The front office was dark and no lights shone from the L-shaped units grouped about the swimming pool, or from the gas station and café next door. Hale settled down to wait, watching the narrow road and checking his revolver.

"Revolver?" Osgood frowned. "Isn't that a bit primitive? One would at least expect some sort of death ray—"

Hale ignored the sarcasm. "Naturally we have our own weapons. But if someone discovered a melted body that disintegrated at a touch, it might cause a certain amount of comment. Secrecy was the vital consideration and death from a bullet wound was the safest method; it would look like just another gangland slaying.

"You see the implications, of course. The Don is killed by a shot from an invisible source. No one knows who fired the weapon. There is confusion, then panic. The mafiosi flee—but from that moment on, fear becomes their constant companion. Who killed the Don? Who is the traitor in their ranks? And who will be the next to die?

"Others would die soon enough. I'd have the license numbers of the cars: tracing them, I'd pick off the *capiregime* one by one. Morale would collapse, there'd be total disintegration. That's when the *hetchors* would send others like myself—hatched and trained to take over the power structure of the organization as visible, apparently human leaders. But it would all begin with the revolver I held in my hand as I waited."

Arthur Hale huddled in the bushes for a long time as the sun rose, the birds twittered, the insects buzzed and circled in the tall grass.

Then the cars began to arrive—the flashy foreign sports models of the young hoods, the modish Mercedeses of the executive echelon, the conservative Caddies and Continentals of the elderly Mustache Petes.

Dutifully Hale noted the numerals on the license plates of a dozen states, eagerly he scanned the faces of the figures emerging from each vehicle. Which one of these men was the Don?

He had no clue. But by noon the motel driveway and parking area was choked with cars, and no more appeared.

Each passenger had entered the motel office, then proceeded to one of the units behind it. And now, on the stroke of twelve, the guests came forth and trooped into the little café next door.

Hale waited until all had gone inside, then rose and crossed the road.

Invisibly, undetectably, he edged the door ajar and entered the café, revolver poised and ready.

For a moment he stood there in the doorway, eyes scanning the room. Where was the Don?

The café was crowded with circular tables covered by red-and-white checkered cloth and already heaped high with bottles, bowls of salad, and platters of pasta.

Every table was occupied by four or five diners, and from each arose a polyglot babble of cultured accents, street vernacular, fluent Italian, Sicilian dialect.

Portly and paunchy middle-aged men in business suits were seated buttocks-cheek by jowl with long-haired youths in trendy outfits; flashily dressed sporting types gesticulated with diamond-studded fingers; burly oldsters with no apparent neckline between bullethead and beefy body stared stolidly at their plates as they forked food into moving mouths.

But who was the Don?

"It was then," said Arthur Hale, "that I realized I must rely on tradition. The grand tradition of humbleness and humility to one's superiors.

"And as I stood there, watching and waiting, I found my answer.

"For now, from time to time during the meal, various men rose from their seats. One by one they moved quietly and unobtrusively to the swinging door at the far end of the café—the door leading to the kitchen.

"I had noticed two waiters entering and leaving that kitchen with trays of food. Suddenly I realized that only when those waiters were here in this room did anyone quit a table and venture through the swinging door. Their disappearance was always brief, their return swift—before the waiters left again.

"Now both waiters were here, in the café. And for a moment no one had risen to pass through to the kitchen beyond.

"Quickly, I made my move. Threading invisibly between the tables, I reached the swinging door.

"Now came the moment of risk. I had to open that door without detection.

"I stood there, hesitating, glancing around the crowded café until I made certain—as surely as I could—that no one was directing his gaze toward the door.

"Then, gripping the revolver, I eased my way through and darted into the kitchen.

"It was a hot and steamy little room, reeking of garlic, fettucine, and the scent of peppers which rose from the pots and cauldrons simmering on the huge old-fashioned wood stove at its center.

"And it was deserted.

"No kitchen help stood at the serving counter, no scullery men were at the sink. No cook presided over the big stove.

"I stared, perplexed, gazing across the kitchen in utter confusion. Through the swirling vapor rising from the stove I saw a pantry entrance at the far end.

"Now, through that entrance, the cook appeared. Not a fat and jolly mustachioed man in a tall chef's hat—just a little wizened figure in a wrinkled black suit, with a soiled white apron tied around his waist. He shuffled into the room carrying a jar of tomato sauce. Moving to the stove, he opened the jar and prepared to dump its contents into a pasta pot.

"Was this the Don—this tiny wrinkled old man cooking spaghetti in the kitchen of a cheap café? Would the overlord of the organization hide away here in the wilderness, living in simple obscurity as he ruled the powers that controlled the world?

"At first glance, at first thought, it was obviously impossible.

"But on second thought—why not? What better cover, what better disguise than this? When one has power—*real* power over life and death and destiny—one can relish it without riches.

"Second thought demanded a second glance. As the little old man stood over the stove I moved closer.

"And it was then that he looked up. He looked up, and for a moment I saw his eyes; deep, dark, glittering like ink-black ice.

"As I stared into those eyes I knew that this was indeed the Don.

"And he was staring at me.

"I knew he didn't *see* me—he couldn't possibly see me—but something about that glittering gaze revealed his awareness of my presence.

"Still watching those eyes, I raised the revolver. And that was my mistake.

"Because I should have been watching his hand instead—his hand, moving in a blinding blur as he lifted the jar of tomato sauce and splashed its contents over my body.

"The invisible sheath extended, of course, to my clothing and to the weapon I held. But whatever splashed against it would be seen—and now my red and dripping face and arms were suddenly and clearly outlined to his vision.

"It was then, as I reeled back to wipe the stinging liquid from my eyes, that the little old man pulled a pistol from under his apron and shot the revolver out of my hand.

"I fell to the floor. But just before I fainted I caught a final glimpse of the Don standing over me.

"Standing. Shimmering. And disappearing."

Arthur Hale sighed. "You know the rest," he said. "The shot must have scared the mob in the café. They'd all taken off by the time the sheriff arrived and found me lying alone and unconscious on the kitchen floor.

"There'd been no question of rescue: my people had monitored the proceedings and when I failed them they left for good. My invisibility ended with the introduction of a foreign body— the bullet which pierced my hand.

"So I was still in the infirmary of the county jail when the Feds came by and picked me up. After that all I could do was make the kind of noises which would bring me here to you."

"Why me?" I said.

"Because you're the head of the Bureau. You're the only one in a position to help."

"Against the Mafia?"

"You don't understand. They're *not* Mafia. Not the top leaders, anyway. The little old man is one of them, but there must be others.

"Others who had the same idea we Vespixians did. Extraterrestrial life forms who came here in vessels of their own, realized who controlled the world, and gradually infiltrated into Mafia ranks just as we planned to do.

"They must have the same powers of invisibility and the same purpose. But they got here first and now they rule." Hale's voice rose shrilly. "You've got to stop them, don't you see that? Find them and destroy them before it's too late—"

Dr. Osgood had already pressed the buzzer and now the security officer was back in the room, yanking at the metal chain and pinioning Hale's arms. Hale was still threshing and screaming as he was dragged out into the corridor.

Osgood listened as the echoes died away, then shrugged. "Poor devil! Talk about paranoid fixations—"

"You'd better look after him," I said.

"Yes. He'll need sedation."

Osgood started for the door, opened it, then stood hesitating on the threshold. "You don't think— Could there possibly be some distorted element of truth in what he told us?"

"Invisible Vespixians and disappearing Mafia?" I shook my head. "No, I don't think."

Osgood went out, closing the door behind him.

For a moment I sat back. But as I had told Osgood, I wasn't thinking. There was no need to think, because the answer was obvious.

It was just an example of the law of averages at work.

What did the astronomers and astrophysicists say? Out of millions of galaxies and billions of solar systems, there had to be thousands of planets capable of supporting life—thousands with life forms more intelligent than those on earth.

Given this possibility, it was quite conceivable that Vespixian aliens could come here bent on conquest. And discover that a similar alien race had preceded them with the same purpose, even using the same method of invisibility to attain their goal.

It was strange, though, that both had arrived at the identical conclusion about the Mafia being the real rulers.

Apparently neither had considered another possibility—that the true secret might lie within the established government itself. Not with dictators and presidents but with those behind them; the shadowy organization of secret police and official espionage agencies who operate above the law and who, by blackmail and intimidation, control the public figureheads.

Theirs was the real power in the world today.

I glanced at my watch. The entity which called itself Arthur Hale would be back in his cell by now and Osgood would be administering an injection. This would be the best time, when they were still together.

Rising, I opened the desk drawer and took out my revolver.

I moved to the door.

And disappeared.

But First These Words—

On the morning of January 5, 1976, at precisely 10:18 A.M., a man named Charlie Starkweather received a visit from God Almighty.

Since Charlie happened to be one of the senior copywriters with the prestigious advertising agency of Pierce, Thrust, Hack, and Clobber, Inc., God had a hell of a time getting in.

You just don't show up at a top Madison Avenue office without an appointment and expect to get past the receptionist unless you can flash an I.D., so right away there was a problem. In an age where everyone is expected to carry a driver's license, a Social Security card, and a plastic wallet filled with an assortment of plastic credit cards, God was at a distinct disadvantage: He didn't even have a valid birth certificate. Painful experience had taught Him not to announce Himself by name: He'd merely be dismissed as a religious fanatic.

Nor would more spectacular methods serve as they had in the past. Descending in a fiery cloud or appearing in a burning bush would only result in trouble with the Fire Department.

So in the end, the only way to slip past security was to go right into Charlie Starkweather's head, and that was a mighty uncomfortable place to be on this, the first working day of the New Year.

To begin with, Charlie's head was throbbing with the effects of a postholiday hangover, built up by long weeks of partying. It was also infiltrated by painful twinges of envy and self-pity, owing to the fact that Charlie was the sole senior copywriter actually on duty at the office today.

Ordinarily, the Almighty would have avoided Charlie's head like the plague—and nobody knew more about plagues than He did, having started so many of them—but this time there was no help for it. He had to give Charlie the message.

Charlie was standing at the water cooler when He arrived, trying to convey the contents of a paper cup to his lips with trembling fingers, and irrigating his fly in the process.

"God!" said Charlie.

"Speaking," said the voice in Charlie's head. "And I've got a word for you."

"Why me?" Charlie groaned, dropping the cup.

"Because you believe. If you only knew the time I've had trying to find somebody in the business who still believes!"

Charlie listened, nodding sympathetically from time to time as the voice explained.

"It's the First Commandment," He said. "You remember— *Thou shalt have no other gods before me.*"

"I don't," Charlie murmured.

"But your boss does, and so do the account execs. They worship Mammon. I tried to get into the heads of the FCC, but they're too thick. And nobody can reach your clients; they're always in conference. That leaves you."

"Leave me where?"

"Here. Listening to me. The time has come to do something about television."

"Why?"

"Because of the Second Commandment. *Thou shalt not make unto thee any graven image, or any likeness of any thing that is in heaven above, or that is in the earth beneath, or that is in the water under the earth. Thou shalt not bow down to them, nor serve them—*"

"Please. You're shouting in my ear."

"Sorry. But you do see the problem, don't you? All these little boxes in darkened rooms all over the earth. Graven images enshrined in every home, with billions of people sitting silently before them, worshipping—"

"People don't worship television. They just watch it."

"And believe what they see. Belief is what leads to worship. Worship of athletes, worship of stars, worship of talk-show hosts. Not heavenly hosts, mind you, but characters like Johnny Carson and Merv Griffin!"

"You're shouting again."

"You're Me-damned right I am. It's about time somebody

shouted. And it's reaching the point where the belief itself is getting worse than the worship. Because people have come to accept television messages as gospel. Even those commercials you write—"

"But that's my job. What can I do about it?"

God told him.

"It won't work." Charlie shook his head and God winced.

"Try," He said. "Now here's what I want you to do."

In the end Charlie staggered back to his desk, sat down before his typewriter, and did it.

Then he took the results in to Mr. Hack. His other bosses, Pierce, Thrust, and Clobber, were on location at a luxury hotel in the Bahamas with a crew of twenty, including six gorgeous models who were part of a two-hundred-thousand-dollar assignment to photograph a thirty-second commercial spot about peanut butter. Mr. Hack, knowing what his partners were up to—and, most probably, into—was in a foul mood. He glared at the piece of paper which Charlie placed on his desk.

"What's this?"

"Little copy synopsis I turned out."

"Who's the client?"

"No client. Sort of a model for a new slant we might use. I've been thinking—"

"You're being paid to write, not to think."

"But it's a new approach. It could revolutionize the whole business."

"Revolutionize? That's Communist talk!"

"Nothing like that, I swear it. If you'll only read—"

"Okay, Starkweather." Mr. Hack sighed, picked up the paper, and scanned it, moving his lips.

Charlie's synopsis was simple. It read as follows:

Mexico City. A hot day in the year 1519. Under the blazing sun a throng of Aztecs gather around the base of a teocatl pyramid. Amid the thunder of drums and the squealing of flutes, the feather-clad priests drag a captive up the stone steps to the altar of sacrifice. As they press their victim down upon the slab, the high priest moves forward, grasping an obsidian knife. The knife is raised—the priest starts to drive it down—then winces, flings it aside, and clutches his shoulder.

One of the other priests looks up and murmurs, "What's the matter—arthritis pain bothering you again?"

The high priest nods—the other priest goes into his pitch—offers him the sponsor's product in a glass of tequila—the high priest drinks—smiles—picks up the knife—rips the victim open—plucks out his heart—thrusts it toward CAMERA—and says, "Give to the United Heart Foundation."

Mr. Hack looked up. "Where the hell did you get an idea like this?" He scowled. "Jesus Christ—"

"You're close," Charlie said. "There's a danger that people are taking the commercials too seriously. We've got to change that while there's still time. A touch of humor—don't you see—"

But Mr. Hack didn't see. He kicked Charlie Starkweather out on his assignment.

On the evening of February 27, 1980, Fred and Myrna Hoober were watching *Ah Fong Goo,* an ethnic detective series featuring a Chinese private eye with a new slant on criminal investigation.

During Fred's first beer there was a thrilling chase sequence through the Grand Canyon which wiped out six cars, three dune buggies and a burro. Midway in Fred's second beer the hero went down to the harbor to interrogate the villain. Fred guessed it was the villain, because he had a yacht. As usual, the villain played it cool.

"Okay, so I did wear a Santa Claus suit at the playground," he said. "But that doesn't necessarily prove I'm a child molester."

Fred had finished his second beer and was just reaching for his third when the image faded and a suave announcer's voice informed him that the program would be continued after this important paid political message from Milo T. Snodgrass, candidate for United States senator.

Gulping his beer, Fred listened to Mr. Snodgrass's assurances that, if elected, he would cut government spending, provide millions of new jobs through federal funding, eliminate crime, liberalize gun-control laws, fight pollution, encourage car sales by lowering automobile emission standards, crack down on monopolies, do away with antitrust suits that interfered with business—

Suddenly another voice interrupted the candidate.

"Repent!" it said. "Repent, ye miserable sinners, for the time is at hand. The day of judgment cometh—"

Onscreen, the candidate goggled.

Offscreen, Fred Hoober gargled into his beer. "Huh? What's that?"

"Must be getting interference from another channel," said Myrna. "Maybe Billy Graham—"

She reached out and switched to another station. Luckily, it was showing the eighty-ninth rerun of an old "Lucy" show. They settled down to watch it and Fred opened another beer.

Lucy, in an attempt to discourage prospective buyers of her house by convincing them there was a termite problem, came out in the costume of a giant ant. She opened her mouth to speak, and over her lines a voice murmured something that sounded like "O ye of little faith."

But Fred was belching and didn't hear it.

After that, the voice was silent.

During the afternoon of March 9, 1983, the President of the United States and his principal advisers were holding an emergency summit meeting in a sand trap at the fifth hole of the Clammy Palm Desert Golf Course.

"It's one hell of a problem, Mr. President," said the secretary of state. "What are you going to do?"

The President shook his head. "I don't know. I was thinking of using my four iron—"

"I'm not talking about the next shot," said the secretary. "It's the condition of the nation I'm worried about."

"Forget it." The President frowned. "I didn't drag a staff of ninety people clear across the country in Air Force One just to discuss national affairs. I've got more important matters to consider." He studied his ball. "How do I lie?"

"Exactly," said the secretary of defense. "How *do* you lie? The population's up to a quarter of a billion and we've got fifty million unemployed. We've already boosted welfare payments but it doesn't mean a thing: with this galloping inflation, the dollar isn't worth a plugged nickel. Half the world is at war—with the other half. And the air is so polluted—"

"Air." The President nodded quickly. "That's your answer. Trouble with you fellows, you don't follow what's on the air. Well, I do." He smiled. "I was watching television just last night, waiting to see that new game show, 'You Bet Your Ass,' or whatever it's called—and I accidentally switched to a news broadcast. This guy, one of the biggest commentators on the networks, was saying as how the real trouble is all in our minds, just negative thinking. Instead of griping about what's wrong with the world we should remember what's right."

"But he's only a news commentator—"

"What do you mean, *only?*" said the President. "Who knows more about the news than a commentator? That's his business, to tell us what's really going on. And this man is an expert; why, he earns more a year than I do!"

Off in the distant desert a pillar of fire suddenly started to form and flicker, but the smog was so thick that nobody noticed. And when the President swung, sliced, and started to curse, no one heard the voice crying out in the wilderness.

On the night of April 30, 1986, Finnegan's Bar and Grill was crowded. But then it was always crowded and so was everyplace else.

No one was in the grill—that part of the operation had been closed for months because of the food shortage—but the bar area was decorated with wall-to-wall people. Not your upwardly mobile elitist types, but plain, ordinary folks who appreciated the informal atmosphere of a genuine replica of an old-fashioned tavern, an authentic imitation of a corner barroom located on the eighty-second floor of a brand-new high-rise savings-and-loan building.

Some customers were drinking, some were smoking, some were sniffing, some were mainlining, and a few diehards were just crouching in the corners under the air-conditioning vents, trying to inhale a breath of fresh, clean recycled smog.

But everyone was here for a good time, and a little crowding didn't matter. Sure, ten grand was a steep price to pay for a shot and a chaser, but the alcohol killed the germs in the water, and if you didn't drink you could always turn on.

Turn on the transistor radios and hear that new rock group,

the Dow-Jones Industrials, getting into their big platinum-record hit, "Up the Creek Without a Snorkel."

Turn on the TV to the educational channel and watch the Triple-X-Rated Movie of the Week, "King Kong Meets Deep Throat."

Sure, there were a few rip-offs, several muggings, an occasional gang rape, and a couple of teenies who cornered an old man in the washroom and flushed him to death. But, as the announcer was saying on the government commercial that interrupted the movie, sex and violence were under control. The bulk of the customers here were just like the everyday crowd at—

"The Tower of Babel!"

The voice rising above the din was almost audible, but only for a moment. Because somebody had just opened a window, and now all you could hear was street noise—cars crashing, ambulance sirens wailing, homemade bombs exploding, rioters screaming, and the drone of police fighter planes overhead. After all, it *was* Saturday night.

"Generation of vipers," said the voice, talking to Itself. "This time no Flood, no Ark, no Noah—I swear it! Now where did I stockpile those thunderbolts—?"

The world ended on May 17, 1988. But the Lakers were playing an important game, and nobody even noticed.

Picture

Farley found the devil through the Yellow Pages.

Of course he had to make inquiries first. He haunted the reserved section of the public library until he found an old book containing the right spells. Then he shopped around for chalk and candles and a lot of smelly herbs. By the time he had drawn a pentagram and set the candles out and burned the herbs Farley was pretty beat.

Next he chanted the spells and conjured up Astaroth—a rather ugly customer who rode a dragon, carried a viper in his left hand, and seemed very uptight about being disturbed.

But Farley kept safely inside the pentagram and told him what he wanted.

Astaroth shook his head. "Not my department," he said. "You'll have to talk to the boss."

"And where can I find him?"

"Locally he goes by the name of Dr. Horner. He's in the book."

"Can I tell him you sent me?"

"Tell him and be damned," said Astaroth. "I'm getting the hell out of here."

And he did.

It took Farley two days just to air out the place afterward, and he had a rough time squaring things with the landlady when she complained about the noise. But finally he picked up the phone book and located Dr. Horner's name.

Not too surprisingly, he turned out to be a Beverly Hills psychiatrist.

Getting an appointment was a hassle; the receptionist did a number about being all booked up until a year from next Thursday. Then he mentioned Astaroth's name and it turned out to be the magic word.

"Come in tonight," she said. "Ten o'clock."

So finally Farley found himself in the private office, face to face with Astaroth's boss.

Dr. Horner turned out to be elderly and a bit on the short side. The eyes peering from behind heavy glasses seemed quite normal and there were no unnatural growths sprouting from his forehead.

"You don't look like the devil," said Farley.

Dr. Horner blinked. "You don't look like a man suffering from delusions," he said. "But of course when my receptionist mentioned Astaroth I knew it was my professional duty to see you as quickly as possible. Would you like to talk about your problem?"

"I'm frustrated," said Leo Farley.

"Aren't we all?" Dr. Horner nodded. "Taxes, inflation, wholesale corruption, retail violence. And on top of everything else, this damned business about malpractice insurance." He broke off abruptly. "Sorry," he said. "Suppose you sit down and tell me."

So Farley told him. About his unhappy childhood—not making top grades in school, not making the team, not making girls. How the war in Nam kept him from college, and how he couldn't enroll when he returned. His parents died in a car crash and he had to go to work in a paint store, even though he was allergic to turpentine.

Then he got into his marriage. Margaret wasn't much for looks and she couldn't cook anything but TV dinners, and though he wanted kids she turned out to be sterile. She was also frigid, a nagger, and a compulsive folksinger. This latter affliction brought about her death from hepatitis, following the purchase of a secondhand guitar with an infected pick.

So for the past six months Leo Farley had lived alone, a pudgy middle-aged man whose hair—since he was not a politician—was turning gray. He still worked at the paint store, still ate TV dinners, and it seemed as though all he got out of life was older.

"Ever thought about suicide?" asked Dr. Horner.

"Frequently," said Farley. "Is that your best offer?"

Dr. Horner shook his head. "I'm not suggesting—just wondering. With all the rotten luck you've had through the years, what kept you going?"

"This," said Farley.

He opened his wallet and took out the picture.

Dr. Horner squinted at it through his thick lenses. The three-by-three photo was obviously old and the color was slightly faded, but even so there was no denying the beauty of its subject. The teenage girl posing full length in a brief bikini had a voluptuous figure and a sensual, provocative face framed by an aureole of flaming red hair.

The psychiatrist reacted with an unprofessional but highly appreciative whistle. "Who is she?"

"Linda Duvall," said Farley. "That's how she looked when she won the beauty contest back in high school. Actually she was even prettier. I cut this picture out of the annual."

"Your girlfriend?"

"I never even met her." Farley sighed. "She only dated jocks. The football team, the basketball team, the track team, guys like that. And, of course, the substitutes."

"Promiscuous, eh?"

"I prefer to think of her as democratic," Farley said. "Though that's just a wild guess. Like I say, I didn't know her."

"But you had a schoolboy crush on her, right?"

"Wrong. A man doesn't carry a picture of a girl in his wallet for twenty years just because of an adolescent hang-up. I've looked at it night and day and it still drives me up the wall."

"I see," said Dr. Horner. "So that's why you came to me. You want to get rid of those erotic fantasies."

"No. I want you to make them come true."

Dr. Horner stared at Farley for a long moment. "Then you really did see Astaroth?"

"That's right. And he said you were the boss."

"Astaroth has a leaky mouth." Dr. Horner frowned. "But suppose I could help; are you prepared to pay the price?"

"Anything you ask. Just get me Linda Duvall."

"What do you intend to do with her?"

Farley explained in detail.

"My, my," said Dr. Horner. "I hope you're up to it! That's a pretty heavy schedule for just one night."

"One night?" Farley scowled. "But I was thinking more along the lines of seven years—"

Dr. Horner shrugged. "Sorry, that's the old contract. We don't use it anymore. In the old days, with only a few clients—people like Faust, you know—we could afford to give them personal attention. But now there's just too many deals to keep track of. I'm afraid one night is all I can offer."

Farley picked up the picture of the red-haired girl and studied it. The sound of heavy breathing filled the room. "I've got to have her," he said. "*Got* to."

Dr. Horner smiled. "I understand."

"Do you?"

"Of course. They don't call me Old Horny for nothing." He reached into a desk drawer and produced a parchment covered with crabbed handwriting. "Sign here," he said.

Farley's eyes narrowed as he scanned the document. "I can't read Latin."

"Too bad. It's really the only civilized language." Dr. Horner shook his head. "You needn't worry, though; it's a standard contract. Covers everything except acts of God. We have the services of some pretty big attorneys."

"That figures," said Farley.

"What's bugging you then? If it's the sight of blood, don't worry. We can dispense with that formality." Dr. Horner held out a pen. "Here. All I want is a legal signature."

Farley took the pen, then hesitated once more.

"Now what?" said Dr. Horner.

"I'll level. You have a reputation for cheating on your bargains."

"That's a damnable lie!" Dr. Horner said. "I'm not a crook."

"Seems to me I've heard that before," Farley told him.

Dr. Horner shook his head. "You're getting a fair deal. One night with the girl in the picture, Linda Duvall. How could I cheat you?"

"Lots of ways," Farley said. "I tried to locate her myself, you know, but I came up with zilch. And then I realized twenty years must have changed Linda as much as they've changed me. Suppose you find her and I end up with a fat, middle-aged klutz?"

"She won't be, I promise you."

"For all I know she might even be dead. I don't want a revived corpse, either."

Dr. Horner chuckled. "Don't worry. She won't be dead, and

she won't be a day older or younger than she is in the picture. And to anticipate your other objections, I also guarantee that she won't be mentally or physically ill, she won't be frigid, and she won't be a lez. Tell you what I'll do: just to sweeten the deal, I'll make her a virgin."

"Yeah." Farley licked his lips, then frowned again. "But suppose she hates me?"

"I'll take care of that, too. I give you my word she'll be just as eager as you are."

"You won't make me impotent?"

"What a suspicious mind you have!" Dr. Horner beamed at Farley appreciatively. "I promise you'll be able to perform indefinitely. And definitely, too."

"Then what happens?"

"I'll come for you at dawn."

"But we'll have the night together?"

"Assuredly."

"Just as she is here?" Farley pointed at the picture.

"Exactly."

Farley gripped the pen and signed.

Dr. Horner picked up the parchment and put it back in his desk drawer. "There we are," he said.

"But where is she?"

Dr. Horner smiled. "Linda is waiting for you now—in your apartment."

Leo Farley smiled then too, for the first time. "I hate to eat and run," he said. "Or vice versa. But if you'll excuse me—"

"By all means." Dr. Horner waved Farley to the door. "Drive carefully," he said.

Farley drove very carefully.

One thing he had to say for himself: he was always careful. That's why he'd taken such pains to make sure about the contract; he had no intention of being outwitted. As a matter of fact, he was a little surprised that the devil didn't have more smarts. The truth was that Farley had cheated *him*.

Now, driving home, it was his turn to chuckle when he thought of how his life story had gone down so easily. Because it hadn't really been such a bummer after all.

His childhood was never unhappy; his parents spoiled him rotten and he was always the biggest bully in the neighborhood. The only reason he didn't do well in school was that he preferred goofing off to studying. He could have been on the football team if he wanted, but he used his time to set up a betting pool instead and made a bundle off his fellow students. His service in Nam was a crock: he'd spent all his time in Saigon as a company clerk by day and a black market operator by night, which got him an even bigger bundle. And when gambling wiped him out, his parents' death left him a nice chunk of inheritance after he returned. Sure, he'd worked in the paint store, but actually as a silent partner who got 50 percent of the take. With the chicks through the years he got 100 percent of the action. And that's what really blew his marriage, when Margaret found out. Slipping her the infected guitar pick was his own idea; it solved all his problems.

Except for Linda Duvall. That part—about the twenty years of frustration—was true. He had the hots for her in school, he had the hots for her all these years, and he had the hots for her now. She was the only thing he wanted that he hadn't been able to get—but he was getting her tonight.

Farley grinned. He'd already damned himself a dozen times over, so there'd been no need for the devil to make such a bargain. Farley had ripped him off.

Just to make sure, he reviewed the terms of the contract, but he found no loopholes. He was going to get just what he asked for—Linda Duvall, the way she was in her picture, alive, willing, eager. And then—

The mere thought of what was going to happen then set his heart pounding as he parked the car, set his hands trembling as he unlocked the apartment door, set his blood racing as he entered.

But the living room was silent and empty.

For a moment Farley wondered if the devil had lied to him after all. Then he saw the light in the hall, streaming forth from under the bedroom door.

Of course—that's where she'd be waiting for him. Well, she wouldn't have to wait long.

He ran down the hall, flung the door open, entered.

And there she was.

Farley stared at her. Linda Duvall, in the flesh—a gorgeous redhead, stark naked, sprawled across the bed and smiling up at him in invitation.

The devil hadn't lied; she was as pretty as a picture. In fact she was just like her picture.

Leo Farley turned away with a sob and stood waiting for the dawn. There was really nothing else he could do.

Not with a girl who was exactly two inches tall.

The Undead

E very evening at six Carol took off her glasses, but it didn't
seem to help. In the old movie reruns on TV, Cary Grant was
always there to exclaim—with a mixture of surprise and gentle-
manly lust—"Why, you're beautiful without your glasses!"

No one had ever told Carol that, even though she really was
beautiful, or almost so. With her light auburn hair, fair skin, regular features and sapphire-blue eyes, she needed only the benefit of
contact lenses to perfect her image.

But why bother, when Cary Grant wasn't around? The book-
shop's customers for first editions and rare manuscripts seemed
more interested in caressing parchment than in fondling flesh.

And by nightfall the place was empty; even its owner had
departed, leaving Carol to shut up shop, lock the doors, and set
the alarms. With a valuable stock on hand she was always mindful of her responsibility.

Or almost always.

Tonight, seated in the rear office and applying her lipstick
preparatory to departure, she was surprised to hear footsteps
moving across the uncarpeted floor in the hall beyond.

Carol frowned and put her compact down on the desktop. She
distinctly recalled turning out the shop lights, but in her preoccupation with self-pity could she have forgotten to lock the front
entrance?

Apparently so, because now the footsteps halted and a figure
appeared in the office doorway. Carol blinked at the black blur of
the body surmounted by a white blob of head and hair.

Then she put on her glasses and the black blur was trans-
formed into a dark suit, the white blob became the face of an
elderly gentleman with a receding hairline. Both his suit and his
face were wrinkled, but the old man's dignified bearing over-

shadowed sartorial shortcomings and the onslaughts of age. And when he spoke his voice was resonant.

"Good evening. Are you the proprietor of this establishment?"

"I'm sorry," Carol said. "He's already left. We're closed for the night."

"So I see." The stranger nodded. "Forgive me for intruding at this late hour, but I have traveled a long way and hoped I might still find him here."

"We open tomorrow at ten. He'll be here then. Or if you'd like to leave a message—"

"It is a matter of some urgency," the old man said. "Word has reached me that your firm recently came into the possession of a manuscript—a manuscript which supposedly disappeared over seventy years ago."

Carol nodded. "That's right. The *Dracula* original."

"You know the novel?"

"Of course. I read it years ago."

Reaching into his pocket the stranger produced an old-fashioned calling card and handed it to her. "Then perhaps you will find this name familiar."

Carol peered at the lettering. The Gothic typescript was difficult to decipher and she repeated aloud what she read. "Abraham Van Helsing?"

"Correct." The old man smiled.

Carol shook her head. "Wait a minute. You don't expect me to believe—"

"That I am the namesake of my great-grandfather, Mynheer Doctor Professor Van Helsing of Amsterdam?" He nodded. "Oh yes, I can assure you that *Dracula* is not entirely a work of fiction. The identity of some of its characters was disguised, but others, like my illustrious ancestor, appeared under their own names. Now do you understand why I am interested in the original manuscript?" As he spoke, the old man glanced at the safe in the far corner. "Is it too much to hope that you have it here?"

"I'm sorry," Carol said. "I'm afraid it's been sold."

"Sold?"

"Yes. The day after we sent out our announcement the phones

started ringing. I've never seen anything like it; just about every customer on our mailing list wanted to make a bid. And the final offer we got was simply fantastic."

"Could you tell me who purchased the manuscript?"

"A private collector. I don't know his name, because my boss didn't tell me. Part of the deal was that the buyer would remain completely anonymous. I guess he was afraid somebody would try to steal it from him."

The old man's frown conveyed a mingling of anger and contempt. "How very cautious of him! But then they were all cautious—concealing something which never truly belonged to any of them. That manuscript has been hidden away all these years because it was stolen in the first place. Stolen from the man to whom the author gave it in gratitude for providing him with the basis of the novel—my own great-grandfather." He stared at Carol. "Who brought this to your employer?"

"He didn't tell me that, either. It's very hush-hush—"

"You see? Just as I told you. He must have known he had no right to possess it. Thieves, all of them!"

Carol shrugged. "Really, I didn't know."

"Of course. And I'm not blaming you, my dear young lady. But perhaps you can still be of some assistance to me. Did you happen to see the manuscript before it was sold?"

"Yes."

"Can you describe it?"

"Well, to begin with, it wasn't called *Dracula*. The handwritten title was *The Undead*."

"Ah yes." The old man nodded quickly. "That would be the original. What else can you recall about it?"

"The cover page was in Bram Stoker's handwriting, but the manuscript was typed. The author's changes and editorial corrections were done by hand, and so was the renumbering of the pages. It looked as though a lot of pages had been omitted—almost a hundred, I'd guess." Carol paused. "That's really just about all I remember."

"And more than enough. From your description there's no doubt it is the genuine manuscript." The old man nodded again. "You're sure about pages being omitted?"

"Yes, quite sure, because my boss commented on that. Why, is it important?"

"Very. It seems Bram Stoker was wiser than his informant. Although the published novel does refer to Count Dracula's plan to bring vampirism to England, this motive is not stressed. What the missing pages contained is what Van Helsing revealed about Dracula's ultimate goal—to spread vampirism throughout the world. They also presented factual proof of Dracula's existence, proof too convincing to be ignored. Stoker wrote down everything Van Helsing told him but had second thoughts about including it in his final draft. I wished to make certain, however, that those pages didn't still exist in manuscript form. Now that I know, it won't even be necessary to seek out the new owner."

"But you talk as though all this was true," Carol said. "It's only a novel. And Count Dracula gets killed in the end."

"Again an example of Stoker's caution," the old man told her. "He had to invent a death scene to reassure his readers. Even so, just think of the influence that novel has had on millions of people who learned of Dracula and vampirism through the book and the theater and films. As it is, many of them still half believe." The resonant voice deepened. "What do you think would have happened if Stoker hadn't novelized the story—if he'd written it for what it was, a true account of the actual experiences of Abraham Van Helsing? Even in novel form, if those missing pages still existed their message might bring a warning to the world which would endanger Dracula's plans."

Carol glanced at her watch as he spoke. Six-thirty. She was getting hungry and the old man's hangup was getting on her nerves. She stood up, forcing a smile.

"This has been very interesting," she said. "But I really must close up now."

"You have been most kind." The old man smiled. "It seems a pity you do not entirely believe me, but I speak the truth. Count Dracula is as real as I am."

Carol reached for her open compact on the desk. In the oval mirror she saw her reflection, but there was none of her visitor, even though he was standing quite close. Close enough for her to smell the rank breath, see the whiteness of the pointed teeth, feel the surprising strength of the hands that rose now to imprison her in their implacable grip.

As he forced her head back Carol's glasses dislodged, clattering to the floor, and for a moment her image in the compact mirror was indeed quite beautiful. Then the bright droplets spurted down, blotting it out forever.

Comeback

They say Southern California has no seasons, but don't you believe it.

Hiking down Santa Monica Canyon, I felt autumn in the air. Twilight comes early in October evenings, and the wind off the ocean was clammy cold. As the fog rolled in I squinted through the haze on the hillside where silent houses huddled beneath towering trees, wrapped in a purplish pallor which only fall can bring.

"Looking for someone?"

I halted, blinking at the man who stepped forward from the shadows on the path ahead.

If the air held a hint of autumn, he was a figure out of winter; there was snow in his hair and ice in his eyes. But his frailty offered no threat and his face was creased in a lined and leathery smile.

"Just sight-seeing," I said. "Wife and I moved in down the street the other day, so I'm exploring the neighborhood."

"Waste of time." He shook his head. "Nothing much to see and nobody worth looking at. Everything's run-down here, myself included." Chuckling, he held out his hand. "Ray Vance is the name. What's yours?"

I told him, and our palms met. It was like shaking hands with a snowman.

"Cold hands, warm heart." He grinned. "Get to be my age, your circulation slows down. I'm pushing eighty-seven this November."

"You've got twenty years on me," I said. "Just retired a couple of months ago."

His grin turned wry. "I didn't. They squeezed me out way back in forty-five. Been here ever since." Vance nodded toward the trees. "Like to see my place?"

"I don't want to intrude—"

"Nonsense. Glad to get a look at another human face. What I see in the mirror nowadays isn't much of a consolation."

Again the dry chuckle came as he turned, leading me up a side path to the weed-choked lawn beyond.

The house hidden on the hillside wasn't as old as its owner, and far better preserved, but the pseudo-Spanish structure was an echo from the twenties. And when he opened the front door for me to enter, I walked into yesterday.

I didn't get home until after dark. Peggy was waiting and worried.

"Where on earth have you been?" she said.

"Time-traveling."

"What's that supposed to mean?"

I told her about Ray Vance and his house. "You wouldn't believe it—like something out of *Sunset Boulevard,* only this is for real. Vance was a movie publicity man back in the silent days, worked for all the big studios. After sound came in things started to get tough and finally he called it quits about forty years ago."

"Forty years?" Peg shook her head. "And he's been sitting up there all alone ever since?"

"Not exactly alone," I said. "The place is full of memorabilia— posters, lobby cards, press books, inscribed photos of just about every old-time star you ever heard of. Nothing modern; instead of a TV set he's still got one of those windup Victrolas. Did you know Rudolph Valentino did a song recording? Neither did I, until Vance played it for me. The whole house is like a museum; film buffs would go crazy over the stuff he has there. You've got to see it."

Peg doesn't share my enthusiasm for old movies, so it didn't surprise me when she shrugged. "I can wait," she said.

But she didn't wait long. About a week later Ray Vance left a shakily scrawled note in our mailbox—an invitation to come for dinner on October 18.

Peggy frowned when she read it. "He's got his nerve. Why, he doesn't even know us!"

I nodded. "From what I gather he doesn't know anybody anymore, and it must be pretty lonely for the old boy. Come on, Peg, be a sport; it won't kill us to go. Besides, I'd like to find out more about the old days."

In the end I persuaded her. And as I predicted, it didn't kill us, though the meal was almost lethal—warmed-up TV dinners served in fancy plates that rested like tiny islands on the long table of his huge dining room. And afterward, when we moved into the den for coffee and drinks, I did find out quite a bit about the old days.

Sitting there on grotesquely overstuffed couches under the pink-bulbed light filtering through beaded lampshades, we were *in* the old days.

Framed three-sheets hung from the walls, featuring forgotten films and forgotten players—House Peters in *Raffles the Amateur Cracksman,* Alberta Vaughn in *The Telephone Girl,* and Raymond Griffith in *Time to Love.*

"Knew 'em all," Vance said. "I could tell you stories—"

And he did, while I listened eagerly, Peg sat patiently, and he kept refilling his glass from the bottle on the table.

He held it up to the light, sounding his raspy chuckle. *"Old Taylor,"* he said. "My drinking buddy. But I knew other Taylors back then. Ruth Taylor, before she got the lead in *Gentlemen Prefer Blondes.* And the guy who got a writing credit on Shakespeare's *Taming of the Shrew*—'additional dialogue by Sam Taylor.' Then there was William Desmond Taylor, the biggest of them all."

"I've heard of him," Peggy said. "He was that director who got murdered and nobody ever found out who did it."

Vance shook his head. "I know who killed him."

"You do?"

The chuckle came. "Remember, I handled publicity in those days. Knowing the truth was part of my job. The other part was to keep it out of the papers." He poured himself a drink. "This business about mysterious deaths is all a crock. People like Tom Ince, Paul Bern, Thelma Todd—they were personal friends of mine. Don't think I didn't find out what really happened to them."

I leaned forward. "Then what are you waiting for? Write a book! If you've got the facts they're worth a bundle, and I don't have to tell you what the publicity would do. A thing like that could be a real comeback for you."

He shook his head again. "I told you they were my friends. They trusted me because I respected their privacy, never let them down. And I'm not about to start now."

"But it doesn't matter," Peggy said. "They're all dead."

"And I will be, soon enough." Vance downed his drink. "That still doesn't give me the right to take advantage of our friendship. You don't understand what Hollywood was like in the old days. More of a small town then, and we stuck together—stars, directors, writers, these people were like family. The only family I ever had." He reached for the bottle again, his voice slurring. "Now there's nothing left but this."

Peggy rose, glancing at her watch. "I think it's time to go," she said.

Vance protested, but I didn't say a word; once Peg makes up her mind, that's it.

We moved into the vestibule and there our host halted and reached for a black leather-bound volume resting on the end table. "Can't let you leave without signing the guest book," he said.

Turning the yellowed pages he reached for a pen. First I signed, then Peggy. As she did so, I noted her sudden but quickly suppressed surprise.

But it wasn't until we got home that I found out what had startled her.

"His guest book," she said. "Did you see the listings? The date on the last signature before we signed was 1959. Nobody's visited him for twenty-five years!"

As far as I know, nobody visited Vance in the days that followed. When I suggested looking in on him, Peggy put her foot down. "Forget it! That place of his gives me the creeps. And no, I don't want him here, either. The way he keeps talking about dead people—it makes me feel as if I was in a graveyard."

"Speaking of graveyards," I said. "Do you know what tonight is?"

She nodded. "Halloween. All the goblins and ghosts will be

out, but I'm ready for them." Peg gestured toward a heap of candy bars on our hallway table.

"You've got enough there for an army," I said. "I'll bet Vance isn't prepared for trick or treat. Why don't I just take some of this junk over to him now?"

Peggy shrugged. "If you need an excuse to see him, suit yourself. Though why you're so worried about that old lush is beyond me."

I didn't know the answer, but I felt my concern growing as I walked up the path in the gathering dusk and knocked on Vance's front door.

For a moment I stood in silence, and my heart missed a beat. All I could think of was the possibility that his heart had missed a beat too. A man that old, feeble and alone, living in the past and dying in the present—

But the man who opened the door was very much alive. Preserved in alcohol, I gathered, catching a whiff of his breath as I explained my errand and handed him the bag of candy.

"Thanks for thinking of me," he said. "Look, I'd ask you in, but I've got to get things ready for tonight."

"Tonight?"

He nodded. "Had a little accident the other day. Nothing serious, but I got the message. Next month I'm moving into the Motion Picture Home."

"Good idea."

"It stinks." His hoarse chuckle terminated abruptly in a coughing spell.

I stared at him as he clutched the doorframe. "Are you sure you're all right?"

"No." Then, surprisingly, he grinned. "That's why I'm throwing a Halloween party. Invited all the old-timers I could think of for one last hurrah."

"Look, if you need any help—"

"Much obliged, but I can manage. Thanks again for thinking of an old man."

I thought of him a lot during the evening, after it got dark and the fog settled in. There weren't as many trick-or-treaters as we'd expected, and no traffic on the street.

"If Vance is having a party," Peg said, "how come we don't see any cars?"

"Maybe everybody walked up."

I said it, but I didn't really believe it. And when Peggy opened the front door and peered up the street, I knew that she didn't believe it either. "Just as I thought," she told me. "No sound, no lights, and no party. You ask me, the old buzzard just flipped out." Then she softened. "Do you think maybe you ought to take a look—?"

It was midnight when I hurried up the hill, moving through the mist toward the dark and silent house. There were no cars parked before it, no marks of tire treads in the driveway, and no response came when I knocked. I pushed the door open and entered the hall.

Vance was lying on his back in the shadows. He'd had another accident, and this time it was a big one. Dialing the paramedics, I knew there wasn't a chance. The only thing that puzzled me was the smile on his face.

I told Peg what had happened after it was all over and I came home again. She listened, her eyes narrowing.

"What's that you've got under your coat?"

I shrugged and pulled it out. "His guest book. Picked it up off the end table before the paramedics arrived."

"You stole it?"

"It wasn't really stealing. You know as well as I do, they'd only toss it away with all his other stuff. But this is priceless, just for its sentimental value. All those old-time movie names . . ."

I riffled it open to the page we'd signed, then stared. New entries had been added, and I scanned them quickly. The signatures were genuine; I know, because I checked them out against autographed photos later. I didn't have to check the names.

Tom Mix. Alma Rubens. Rudolph Valentino. Thelma Todd. Jean Harlow. Paul Bern. Thomas A. Ince. William Desmond Taylor.

No wonder Vance died smiling; he'd had his Halloween party after all. For though each signature was different, the date which followed was always the same—

October 31—1987.

Nocturne

L isten to me, darling.

You don't mind if I talk now, do you? I'm not sleepy yet, and there's so much I want to tell you. I couldn't before, because I was always afraid.

If that sounds funny to you, I can understand why. When you're young and beautiful there's nothing to be afraid of, is there?

I'm the one who was always getting put down, laughed at, rejected. And because of that I guess I came to the point where I rejected myself. Looking back I can see how that would make me afraid, make me a loner.

But you changed all that. I'm not afraid anymore, and with you beside me the loneliness is gone too.

That's another thing you never had to worry about, darling. People like you are never lonely, because they always have love. You get it from your folks when you're a kid, you get it from friends along the way, and then when you grow up you've got it made. Don't think I haven't noticed—all those jocks, the Big Men on Campus, coming on to you, making their moves. And you smiling, taking it all for granted.

Don't get me wrong, I'm not blaming you. Why shouldn't you take it for granted when that's how it's always been?

The reason I'm telling you this is to try and make you understand how different it was for me. Ever since I can remember I was running scared. And the worst time was at night when everything came together—being afraid because I was all alone in the dark and nobody cared, not even my folks.

I used to lie awake here in bed, crying because of the things Mom said, the things Dad did to hurt me. Looking back now I don't think they tried to make me feel bad on purpose; it's just that they didn't know how sensitive I was. To them, telling me I had a zit on my nose was just a joke. When they called me a klutz it was only their way of reminding me to be more careful. Saying that wearing glasses would keep me from making the team didn't mean they blamed me for it. But at the time it really got to me.

That's what made me afraid the most—when I realized I hated them for what they said, how they laughed. If my very own father and mother didn't care about hurting my feelings, how could I expect better from anyone else? To the other kids, the teachers, I must be ten times worse, so I hated them too. But I didn't want to hate them, I was afraid of hating everybody, so—like the shrink said—I projected my fear on the darkness instead.

Oh yes, I went to a shrink. You didn't know that, did you, darling? My folks never told anyone they sent me, it was a kind of guilty secret, something they were ashamed to admit. Their son going to a head doctor because he cried at night. And wet the bed. What's the matter, a big boy like you, acting like a baby? Grow up, be a man, they told me.

The shrink never said that, of course. He tried to help, I know he did, and after a while I got over the enuresis. That's the word he used, I've always remembered it. I remember a lot of things he told me, the things he taught me. But the main thing he taught me was something he didn't realize. He taught me not to show my feelings.

He thought he cured me of being afraid of the dark, and that's why I could stop seeing him. What really happened was I just stopped talking about the things that scared me. I wanted to please him, please my folks, get a taste of what it was like to be praised instead of blamed.

But all I could taste was the fear.

I'd lie awake in the dark night after night, fighting to keep from trembling. Now, instead of being afraid of hating others, I was afraid of *things*. Things like shadows, the shadows that crawled out of the corners, things like the wind howling outside the window. I'd hide my head under the pillows to shut out the shapes and the sounds, but it never worked.

Because then I'd fall asleep and the dreams came. That's when the wind sounds changed into voices laughing at me, and the shadows turned into faces, all staring eyes and mouths that grinned. Every night they came, and every night I'd wake up screaming.

Please, darling, try to remember I'm not telling you this to frighten you, only to make you understand what it was like for me all these years.

The worst part was that I couldn't say anything to anyone. Now I was an adult and everyone thought I'd outgrown my "little problem."

That's what my folks used to call it, my "little problem." At least they didn't talk to me that way when I got older. Instead it was, "I don't see what a humanities major is going to do for you when you get out of school. Time you started thinking about something practical, a career. Here you are, going on twenty-one already, and you still have no idea what you want to do with your life."

Not true, of course. I knew what I wanted to do. I wanted to crawl into a hole somewhere and die. And if I couldn't manage that, maybe I'd have to do something else. Like committing suicide.

Don't think it hadn't crossed my mind. Nights like this, lying alone in bed here, I even planned the ways. But it was no use, I knew I didn't have the guts to go through with it.

Afraid to live, afraid to die. So I read a lot, listened to music, went to the movies, watched TV. It filled time, but it couldn't fill up my life. For that you need friends, people who care.

Please don't get the wrong impression, darling. It isn't like I just turned my back on everybody. I got to know a lot of people on campus and in my classes, and I tried to make friends with them, but it never seemed to work that way. Nobody wanted to hang out with me, invite me to their parties. I guess I know why. Who cares about a skinny little runt with glasses, somebody who's afraid to look anyone in the eye and stutters when he tries to talk?

You never had that problem, did you? I know, because I was watching. Ever since the day you enrolled in English lit class I used to watch. Only it was more than just watching; I memorized you. The way you looked and walked and smiled and laughed, even little things like brushing the hair back from your forehead before you stood up to answer a question.

I don't suppose you noticed me at all. And I never got up enough nerve to talk to you or even say hello, not with that gang always around you—all those grinning guys with Burt Reynolds mustaches doing their macho numbers. Oh, I can't blame you for liking that attention. It's just that I didn't have a chance, and I knew it.

But I needed someone to care, and for a while I thought my folks might still be the answer. Seeing me graduate *magna cum laude* and all that, maybe they'd change their minds about me.

I remember how excited I was when they phoned and said they were cutting their vacation trip short and coming back in time for graduation ceremonies, and how good it felt driving out to the airport to pick them up.

You know what happened, of course. It was on the news, all over the papers. That damned freak crash, taking off from the stopover in Denver. They never got to see me graduate and I never saw them again, just the closed coffins. Then the funeral, and the lawyer, and settling the estate—but I don't want to talk about it. I'm not looking for sympathy, darling, just trying to make you understand.

At first it looked like things would get better for me, because I inherited enough to live on without worrying about a regular job. And there was nobody to put me down now or boss me around.

But that's what made it so bad. I was all alone, rattling around in this big house with no one to see or talk to. I got to feeling like I was in solitary confinement, and maybe I went a little stir-crazy.

That's the only way I can explain what I did. Up to now I've been ashamed to tell anyone, but I can tell you. Maybe you've already guessed the reason I had.

It's because I'd never been with a woman.

Hard to believe in this day and age, isn't it? Twenty-three years old and still a virgin.

So I went to this hooker.

It happened because I couldn't stand being alone anymore, so one night I drove over to this bar. That's another thing: I never did dope and all I'd ever had to drink up until then was a beer or two once in a while. But this time I thought to hell with it, I'm going to find out what it's like, and of course the straight shots hit me right away.

I didn't even know I was drunk, just felt relaxed, almost like I am with you now. I was all alone in the place and I got to talking to the bartender. I don't remember exactly what I said or how it came up, but he told me about this hooker and gave me the address. He even phoned to let her know I was coming; I suppose they had some kind of an arrangement.

If it wasn't that I was drunk I'd never have gone through with it, but I went up to her apartment and she was waiting for me. She was a lot younger and prettier than I expected, more like a high-class call girl. Looking back now I can see she must have known what the situation was and did her best to make things easy, even helping me get my clothes off, and then—

And then, nothing. I won't go into the gory details, I don't want to think about it even now, but everything went wrong, and I couldn't, and she started to laugh and called me a name. I didn't care, all I wanted was out of there.

It wasn't until later that I thought about the name she called me. Then I got mad, but I was really angry at myself for being such a fool.

The only thing I got out of it was learning how the drinks could help. I bought some whiskey to keep in the house and did my drinking at home. Don't worry, I'm not an alcoholic or anything like that. I can quit whenever I want, and I know how to handle the stuff. But a few shots make me sleep better, without the dreams. The trouble is, when I'm awake I still get uptight and I have to take a couple of drinks just to calm down.

But I won't have to depend on whiskey anymore. Now I have you. I don't know how you feel, but to me it's like a miracle. A dream come true.

Because sometimes even the drinks don't help. Like tonight, when I got so worked up remembering all the bad things and wondering if there was any sense in trying to go on. Sitting here in the house when the storm started, listening to the wind rattling the shutters, looking at the empty bottle on the table, I knew I just had to get out.

I hadn't eaten anything since breakfast so I figured maybe some food would help. The rain was really coming down heavy when I left; it was hard to see ahead and the car kept skidding, so I decided to turn off on the side road and take the long way into town.

That's when it really hit me—driving along the pitch-black road in the storm with no lights anywhere, no traffic, nothing but the woods all around. I guess the drinks were hitting me too, because when the fog started to roll in I got this terrible empty feeling inside, as if I was all alone and lost in the middle of nowhere. And I knew that even if the storm stopped and the fog lifted I would still be alone, still be lost, and nothing would ever happen to save me.

Then you happened, darling. You saved me.

The moment I saw you standing there next to that silly little red convertible and waving your flashlight, it was as though everything changed. Just recognizing you, knowing that you were really there and calling out to me, turned a nightmare into a dream come true.

Maybe you think it was just chance that made me take the side road so that I'd find you stranded there after your tire blew. But it wasn't chance, darling; it was fate.

Looking back now I can see that it was meant to be.

Driving you to the service station, finding it closed, bringing you here to the house to use the phone, all this was fate too.

And the way you looked at me, the way you smiled, did something I can't explain. For the first time in my life I felt like a real man. And for the first time in my life I could act like a man.

Let me confess something. I lied when I told you the phone was out. It really worked, but I didn't want you to know. What I wanted was to have you here with me, have you and hold you the way a real man holds the woman he loves.

That's what I did and I hope you understand now. I hope you realize what this has meant to me, and that it means something to you too. I knew I loved you too much to force you, so I'm glad it worked out the way it did. Everything just seemed to happen, because it was fate.

You were so wonderful, darling—not like that hooker, not

like the girls who always laughed. I can forget them now, forget the shame and the tears, because I have you. From now on we'll always be together.

Thank you, darling. Thank you for making me happy with the gift of your love.

I only wish now that I hadn't killed you first.

Die—Nasty

As every student knows, it was James David Autry who started it all.

Way back in March 1984, Mr. Autry, condemned to death by lethal injection, petitioned the Texas State Board of Corrections to allow his execution to be televised.

For some inexplicable reason his request was denied. And as a result it wasn't until 1989, after a five-year series of court battles, that the right to show executions on television was finally upheld. The ACLU proclaimed it a major victory for the freedom of the individual, but at first there was scant attention paid to this decision.

Meanwhile, of course, capital punishment was spreading. State laws against it were being repealed in the face of the increasing crime rate and the growing lack of prison facilities. Although billions had been spent to build new jails and penitentiaries, it was impossible to accommodate the great horde of murderers, forcible rapists of women and children, convicted politicians, and other major criminals.

Finally common sense prevailed, and death sentences were carried out on an ever widening scale. And in 1991 the first execution—that of Floyd Scrilch, convicted of aggravated mopery—was televised on a popular cable network. The success of the simple program, filmed by only two cameras set up outside the California gas chamber, caused wiser heads of commercial television to give the matter a second thought.

A month later a second execution was shown on the prestigious news program "30 Minutes"—formerly "60 Minutes," but renamed because of the number of commercials introduced. As expected there was a great deal of public reaction pro and con, but the winning argument proved to be the ratings. A full 55 percent share of the nation's viewing audience watched the show.

The result was an undignified scramble on the part of network executives to secure exclusive TV rights for the carrying out of death penalties in various states. Naturally the largest crime centers—New York, Illinois, Texas, California, etc.—enjoyed the best offers. But even the smaller states such as Rhode Island and Delaware made lucrative deals with local stations.

Initially most of the programs featured gas chambers, hangings, and electrocutions. Through trial and error it was learned that gas chamber programs had little popular appeal; the proceedings were comparatively slow and lacked visual excitement.

Hangings were unpredictable as crowd pleasers; some were completed quickly while others lasted through several commercial breaks. The slower events naturally provided more drama and proved popular with bookmakers specializing in bets on just how long it would take for a given criminal to cease jerking and be pronounced legally dead.

Electrocutions were generally more successful as audience pleasers, combining our national interest in science and mechanical gadgets with the love of spectacle—such as the "special effects" of sparks curling the victim's hair and smoke pouring out of his ears.

In the spirit of competition which made America great, state legislatures began competing for television revenues by introducing new methods of capital punishment or, more accurately, reviving old ones. Death by firing squad enjoyed a brief vogue, embodying as it did the use of colorful uniformed riflemen and the offer of a blindfold to the condemned. The once general offer of a last cigarette to the prisoner was, of course, omitted, since smoking is injurious to one's health.

North and South Dakota, long ignored as lesser states, captured the public fancy by bringing back the guillotine. Its success prompted Alabama to go them one better in presenting a masked headsman with a quaint and picturesque ax.

Naturally the leading networks and stations entered into the spirit of these occasions. Taking their cue from the fact that beer commercials were especially popular on such programs, they introduced a whole new breed of commentators, many of them former sportscasters.

Soon the "instant replay" became a staple of execution televis-ing. Showmanship came into play, featuring exclusive interviews with the condemned just before their sentences were filmed, then interviews with officials, executioners and clergymen, and, finally, dramatizations of the crimes for which the prisoner had paid his penalty.

Nor were youthful audiences neglected. Always important to sponsors and broadcasters alike, the young people who grew up on the "splatter films" of the past two decades constituted a huge market for this form of entertainment. Their once popular pro-gram favorite, "Saturday Night Live," enjoyed a new upsurge in ratings when it began to feature the Execution of the Week and changed its name to "Saturday Night Dead."

As the boom continued, prison officials eager for TV bids searched history for even more colorful and creative attractions. Pennsylvania reenacted the techniques used in the Indian Mutiny or Sepoy Rebellion of 1856: tying the condemned to the mouth of a cannon and "blowing him away." Multiple executions by this method were inaugurated, but ceased when local residents near the prison complained of noise.

Not to be outdone, Ohio introduced the custom of drawing and quartering, in which the prisoner's arms and legs are tied to four horses, which are then lashed to move in opposite directions, with spectacular results to the prisoner's person. This proved to be a bit of a problem, since the SPCA got into the act and promptly forbade the executioners to use a whip on the horses.

Burning at the stake was a favorite in Florida and flaying alive had its share of fans in Tennessee. Arizona gave an exotic oriental flavor to a two-hour special which featured the "Death of a Thou-sand Cuts."

Unfortunately, no one seems to have foreseen the inevitable result of these entertainments. But within just a few years, the number of rapes and murders suffered an alarming decline.

For a time the entire program concept, so popular with view-ers and so lucrative to penologists, broadcasters, and sponsors alike, seemed fated—as they say in television circles—to "go down the tube."

Fortunately the elected officials realized the danger, and,

taking the welfare of the nation's economy to heart, enacted legislation which labeled more crimes as capital offenses carrying the death penalty upon conviction. With the cooperation of farsighted judges who rejected appeals and did away with the old-fashioned system of public defenders, a fresh crop of prisoners soon blossomed on death row. In fact, so many were now available for public appearances that soon even the lowliest independent stations were carrying execution events weekly, then daily.

It is not definitely known to whom credit should go for the idea, but someone in Washington presently arranged to have local culprits thrown to the lions at the National Zoo. Shortly thereafter the Astrodome and various bowls and sports arenas picked up on the possibilities, and the following season saw both baseball and football give way to mass executions involving the talents of lions, tigers, leopards, bears, and other major carnivores, some of whom achieved individual celebrity for their gastronomic feats. Florence, a female polar bear borrowed for the occasion from the Seattle Zoo, won special distinction for devouring—at least in part—no fewer than six prisoners in the course of the annual Super Bowl.

Everyone seemed pleased with this development except the condemned felons. Exercising their God-given rights as citizens, they formed a union and appealed for redress. A compromise was reached, and as a result the animals were barred from program participation in favor of a new and even more amusing diversion: the gladiatorial combat.

At first large numbers of prisoners were employed, using every conceivable weapon except firearms, which were deemed dangerous to the attending officials and the television camera crews. As an additional objection, it was pointed out that filming such a crowd of combatants required a prohibitively expensive amount of equipment, and a great deal of the most impressive and bloodiest action was never recorded, due to the unpredictability of its occurrence.

Thus individual duels-to-the-death took precedence and proved much more satisfactory in the long run, particularly when embellished with attractive partisan girl cheerleaders urging on their personal "favorites." Many of the condemned entered into the spirit of the occasion, spending long hours of practice before their execution date in order to increase their skill with battle-axes, maces, spears, double-edged swords, and other useful utensils. Since they were allowed no armor for protection, they were naturally encouraged to master their talent for mayhem.

But it remained for science, ever the savior of society, to provide the final touch. In less than a year, leading television manufacturers benefited both the national audience and the national economy by introducing a new TV set with a special attachment, directly aimed to provide viewer participation in the capital punishment process.

Now, when one condemned combatant downed or disabled his opponent, he paused for thirty seconds while the folks watching at home could press a simple button on their television control panels. Instantly, with the aid of a complex computer network, viewers all over the nation could register a "thumbs up" or a "thumbs down" verdict to decide the fate of the fallen gladiator. If spared, both he and his victorious foe still suffered death in accordance with the laws of the land, but were first given the special boon of an appearance on *The Tonight Show.*

The successful introduction of such customs in capital punishment had widespread repercussions in other areas of national life. Scholars, lawmakers, and laymen alike turned to a study of other constructive cultural phenomena in the past and found fresh wisdom in the ways and mores of bygone cultures.

The final and natural outcome of this preoccupation resulted in many social and legal changes. And as we are all aware, these changes came about rapidly.

It was in 1998 that we elected our first emperor.

No one can deny that his reign was eminently successful for well over three years, until this country fell to the barbarian invasion.

Now, of course, we are ruled by savages, and unhappy as it seems, it would appear that the good old days of public executions are gone forever.

Sic transit gloria . . .

Pranks

The lights came on just after sunset.

He stood in the hallway near the front door, filling the candy dish on the table with a skill born of long practice. How many times had he done this, how many Halloweens had he spent preparing for the joyful hours of the evening ahead? No use trying to remember; he'd lost count. Not that it mattered, really. What mattered was the occasion itself, the few hours of magic and make-believe one was privileged to share with the children. What mattered was the opportunity, however brief, to enter into the spirit of things, participate in the let's-pretend on the one night of the year when a childless couple could themselves pretend that they were truly no different from the members of the community around them; solid, ordinary citizens who took pride in their homes and their offspring.

Actually it wasn't all pretense; he was proud of this house, and rightly so, for it was he who had designed and created it, right down to the last knickknack and stick of furniture. And they had always loved children.

But truth to tell, it was the make-believe that thrilled him. Maybe they both had a childish streak of their own, dressing up to surprise the youngsters. And part of the fun was surprising one another, for it was an unspoken rule that neither of them ever revealed in advance just what sort of costume they'd be wearing.

Now, hearing her footsteps on the stairs, his eyes brightened in eager anticipation. One year she'd come sailing down the steps in hoop skirts as Scarlett O'Hara, another time she'd gotten herself up as a black-braided Pocahontas, once she'd worn the powdered wig of Marie Antoinette. What would he see tonight—Cleopatra, the Empress Josephine, Joan of Arc?

Leave it to her to fathom his expectations and astonish him

with the unexpected. And that, as she descended into full view, was exactly what she did. For instead of a figure out of film or fiction he beheld a little old lady with a motherly smile, wearing an apron over a simple housedress, as though she had just stepped out of an old-fashioned country kitchen.

"How do you like it?" she said.

For a moment he stared at her, completely taken aback, yet puzzled by the odd familiarity of her appearance. Where had he seen this smiling elderly woman before? Then, suddenly, his gaze darted toward the candy dish on the table and the empty box beside it. And there on the front of the box was his answer: the oval photographic portrait purporting to represent the candymaker herself. Tonight she was Mrs. See.

Now it was his turn to smile. "Marvelous!" he said. "It's hard for me to imagine you as an old lady, but I must say you look the part."

She nodded, pleased with his reaction. "I think the kids will like it. And they certainly should be able to recognize you too, Ben."

He peered at her through the tiny rimless spectacles and patted his paunch. "I hope so. At least I make a better Ben Franklin than last year's Abraham Lincoln. Though I admit I was tempted to try something different for a change. Remember when I did Adolf Hitler—"

"And scared half the children out of their wits?" She shook her head. "Halloween's for fun, not fright. No, I think you made a good choice."

She bustled over to the table, inspecting the mound of chocolates heaped on the candy dish. "I see you've done my job for me."

"That's right." He paused, listening to the sudden chiming of the grandfather's clock beside the stairs. "Half past seven. They should start coming soon."

Then the doorbell rang.

She opened the door and the two of them stood side by side, gazing down at the little ragamuffin in the cowboy outfit as he clutched his crumpled shopping bag and rattled off the time-honored greeting. "Trick or treat," he said.

She stepped back, smiling. "Isn't he adorable?" she murmured.

Then, "Come right in and help yourself. The candy's on the table."

The moment the front door closed, Joe Stuttman turned to Maggie, scowling. "Jesus H. Christ!" he said.

"Now Joe, please!" Maggie sighed. "Don't get yourself upset over nothing."

"You call that nothing?" His scowl and voice deepened. "Those damned costumes must have cost a fortune. I'm not blind, you know; I read the ads. Okay, so most of Angela's witch outfit you made yourself, but why in hell you had to go and buy Robbie that fancy space suit—"

"Simmer down," Maggie told him. "You don't have to pay for it. I've been saving up from my household allowance these past two months."

"So that's it!" Joe shook his head. "No wonder we've been eating so many of those lousy casserole messes lately. I work my tail off down at the shop and all I get to eat is glop because your son has to dress up like a goddamn astronaut for Halloween!"

"*Our* son," Maggie said softly. "Robbie's a good boy. You saw his last report-card; all those A's mean he's really been doing his homework. And he still finds time to help me around the house and do your yardwork for you. I think he deserves a treat once in a while."

"Treat." Joe went over to the coffee table in front of the television set, picked up the six-pack resting there, then yanked out a can of beer. "That's another thing I don't like—this trick-or-treat business. Running up and down the street at night, knocking on doors and asking for a handout. I don't care what kind of a fancy getup a kid's wearing. What he's really doing is acting like some wino on Main Street, a bum mooching off strangers. You call that good behavior? It's nothing but blackmail if you ask me." He thumbed the beer-can tab. "Trick or treat—it's a threat, isn't it? Pay up or else. What are you training Robbie for, to grow up and join the Mafia?"

"For heaven's sake," Maggie said. "You don't have to go on a roll about it. You know as well as I do that trick or treat is just a phrase. People expect kids to ask them for candy or cookies on Halloween, it's just a tradition, that's all. And if somebody doesn't come through with a treat I'm sure neither Robbie nor Angela is going to do anything about it. They'll just go on to another house." She glanced unhappily toward the front door. "I only wish you'd let me put out a few little goodies for the kids who come here."

"No way," Joe said. He took a gulp of beer. "I thought we had that all settled. I'm not wasting my money on a mess of junk food for a bunch of little bastards who dress up in stupid costumes and come banging on my front door."

"But, Joe—"

"You heard me." Joe scooped up the six-pack with his free hand. "Now let's get those lights turned off, quick, before anyone shows up. I'm gonna watch the game on the set in the bedroom, and I don't want any interruptions. That means don't answer the door, do you read me?"

"Yes," Maggie said. "I read you."

Wearily she turned and started down the hallway toward the kitchen as Joe turned the living room lamp off behind her.

Do you read me? What a stupid question! Of course Maggie could read Joe, she'd been reading him like a book these past twelve years. And there were no surprises awaiting her: the stinginess, the rages, the insensitivity to the needs of others, all were part of an old, old story she'd come to know only too well.

Sighing softly, Maggie began to stack the dishes in the sink. As she did so she reminded herself that she had to be fair. Joe did work awfully hard, he did try to protect his family, and as husbands went he was probably better than most. In spite of his faults, Joe was a good man.

And maybe that was the trouble: he was a good man. A man who seemed never to have enjoyed his childhood, and who couldn't share in the fun his own children wanted to enjoy.

So it was up to her to see that they had a little of that fun in their lives. Like tonight—Halloween—a fun time for kids like Robbie and Angela. She hoped they were having a good time; perhaps when they grew up with families of their own they'd still be able to enjoy a harmless holiday.

★

It seemed to take forever for the twins to get ready; Pam's devil costume was too tight and had to be let out at the waist before it could be zipped up in back, and Debbie kept fussing with her clown makeup.

In point of fact, they didn't actually leave the house until almost eight-fifteen, but within three minutes after their departure Chuck and Linda Cooper were in bed.

"Alone at last!" Linda giggled. "My God, you'd think I was some kind of floozy, sneaking around like this and waiting for a chance to hop into the sack the moment the coast is clear."

"Be a floozy," Chuck said. "Come on, I dare you."

"Don't get me wrong." Linda sobered. "You know how much I love the kids, we both do. But lately it seems like we never get a chance, what with their bedroom right next door to ours and those damned mattress springs squeaking. I'm always afraid they can hear us."

"So let them hear." Chuck grinned. "About time they learned the facts of life."

Linda shook her head. "But they're still so young! Maybe I'm too self-conscious, I don't know. It's the way I was brought up, I guess, and I can't help it."

"Look, let's not talk about it now, shall we?" Chuck tossed the covers aside. "I'm not going to spend the next two hours worrying whether or not the bedsprings squeak."

"Sorry," Linda said. "I know how tight things are right now, the way prices keep going up and you not getting that raise until next year. But if we could only afford a new mattress—"

"Buy you one for Christmas. How's about that?"

"Oh, Chuck!" She turned to him, smiling. "Do you really mean it?"

"Course I mean it. One new mattress for Christmas, that's a promise. But right now we've got another holiday to celebrate, remember?" He took her into his arms. "Happy Halloween," he said.

Sometime around nine-thirty Father Carmichael checked his watch. "Getting late," he said. "I really should be going. I thank you both for a lovely dinner and a delightful evening—"

"Come on, Father, what's your hurry?" Jim Higgins reached for the bottle and leaned forward to pour a good two inches of its contents into the priest's brandy snifter. "One for the road, okay?" he said.

Father Carmichael shrugged in mild protest, but Martha Higgins beamed and nodded at him from her chair beside the fireplace. "Please don't rush away. Billy and Pat should be home soon and I know they'd love to see you."

"I'd like that." The priest twirled his snifter, then raised it to drink, smiling as he did so. Then, as he set the glass down again, his expression changed. "Aren't they a little young to be out at this hour?"

"It's trick-or-treat night, don't you remember?" Jim Higgins swallowed brandy in a single swig that emptied his own snifter. "After all, Halloween only comes once a year."

"Praise the Lord for that," Father Carmichael said softly.

Martha Higgins raised her eyebrows. "Don't you approve of trick or treat?"

"A harmless diversion," the priest told her. "But Halloween itself—"

"Now wait a minute." Jim Higgins spoke quickly, glancing at Martha out of the corner of his eye as he did so. "This is a nice friendly little town. You of all people should know that, Father. I realize a lot of parents go along with their youngsters on a night like this, but we talked it over and decided it was time for Billy and Pat to make the rounds alone if they wanted to. Sort of gives them a grown-up feeling and helps them to understand there's nothing to be afraid of."

"Nothing to be afraid of." The priest sighed. Then, conscious of Martha Higgins's sudden frown, he forced a smile. "Don't mind me," he said. "It's the brandy talking."

"What do you mean?" Jim Higgins was frowning too. "What's all this about Halloween? Are you trying to tell us we ought to be afraid of goblins and witches? I thought people stopped believing in that stuff a couple of hundred years ago."

"So they did." Father Carmichael took a hasty sip from his glass. "They stopped believing. But that in itself didn't necessarily stop the phenomena."

"Don't talk like a damned fool!" Jim Higgins said, then halted, his face reddening. "Sorry, Father—no offense—"

"And none taken." The priest nodded. "You're quite right, of course. We're all of us God's fools, and some of us, I fear, are damned. But I spoke as neither, merely in my capacity as a servant of the Church. And though the Church no longer concerns itself with suppressing old wives' tales about pixies and leprechauns, it has not abandoned the fight against true evil. There are still those of us who are ordained to seek out and dispel the unclean and the unholy, or exorcise unfortunates possessed by demons."

"But isn't a lot of that just superstition?" Martha said. "All this nonsense about vampires and werewolves and the dead coming out of their graves? And even if such things were possible, I don't see what it has to do with Halloween. It's just another holiday."

Father Carmichael finished his brandy before speaking. "The real holiday—holy day, that is—will come tomorrow, on the Feast of All Saints. It's then we celebrate Hallowmas in honor of Our Lady and all the martyrs unknown who died to preserve the faith. The faith which Satan abhors, because it affirms the power of Almighty God.

"But Satan too has power. And he chooses to manifest his defiance on the eve of Allhallows by loosing the forces of evil which he commands." The priest broke off, smiling self-consciously. "Forgive me; I didn't mean to start preaching a sermon. And I hope you realize I was just speaking figuratively, so to say."

"Sure thing." Jim Higgins moved to his wife and put his hand on her shoulder. "Just a little Halloween ghost story, right?"

Martha nodded but her eyes were troubled, intent on Father Carmichael as he glanced at his watch again, then rose.

"Time I was leaving," he said. "I take it I'll be seeing you both at mass tomorrow—"

Martha gestured quickly. "But you haven't seen the children yet! They should be here any minute now. Please, Father. Won't you stay?"

The priest hesitated, conscious that the smile had faded from her face as he stared into the troubled eyes.

"Of course," he said. "Of course I'll stay."

Then there was silence, except for the crackle of flames in the fireplace and the faint, faraway ticking of a clock.

Jim Higgins frowned. "Almost ten-thirty," he murmured. "They promised to be back by ten at the latest." The frown deepened. "You'll pardon my language, Father—but where in hell are those kids?"

"Heavenly," Irene Esterhazy said. "I mean heavenly." She lurched against the buffet table as she took another bite of her croissant. "Try one, honey; they're soooo good!"

Howard Esterhazy shook his head. "No time for that," he told her. "We've stayed too long as it is."

"But it's such a lovely party." Irene turned, nodding toward the crowd of couples milling about in the living room beyond, her voice rising above the babble of animated conversation. "Besides, I want 'nother drink—"

She lurched again and Howard gripped her shoulder. "You've had enough," he said. "We're going home."

"Oh, Howie—"

"You heard me." He guided her forward. "Now pull yourself together and say good night to our host and hostess."

Irene made a face. "Must I?"

"You must," Howard said.

And she did, somehow managing not to slur her words as they exchanged farewells and made their way out to the driveway.

Once in the car, with the windows open and the night air fanning her face, Irene sobered slightly. "You mad at me, honey?"

"No." Howard sighed, eyes intent on the road. "I guess you're entitled to a little diversion once in a while. But do you realize what time it is?"

Irene focused her eyes on the illuminated dial of the dashboard clock. "My God, you're right! It's almost eleven. I had no idea—"

Her husband nodded. "I know. And I didn't want to spoil your fun. It's just that I told Connie we wouldn't be late."

"Maybe we ought to give her a little something extra," Irene said. "She's always been so good about sitting with Mark, even though she does play that damn stereo full blast."

"You can say that again," Howard muttered as they pulled up

before the house. The wind was rising, sending surges of sound through the treetops, but the screech of the stereo echoed so loudly that even their voices were drowned by its pounding beat as they left the car and moved up to the front door.

Howard's thumb jabbed at the buzzer. "Maybe I should use the key," he said. "She can't hear anything over that racket."

But as he fumbled in his pocket the door swung open quickly and Connie peered out. "Oh, it's you," she said.

"Who did you expect, Michael Jackson?" Howard scowled.

"I thought it was Mark." Connie's voice faltered.

"Mark?" Irene moved into the hall, her forehead furrowing. "You mean he isn't here?"

"Please, Mrs. Esterhazy." The girl gestured helplessly. "Don't be angry with me. I thought it would be all right." Her voice was muffled by stereophonic stridency.

"Turn that thing off!" Howard shouted.

Retreating to the living room, Connie hastily obeyed, then turned to confront the Esterhazys' accusing stare.

"Now what's all this about Mark?" Howard said. "Where is he?"

Connie's gaze dropped and her words came with forced bravado. "You know Bill Summers, that friend of his from down the street? Well, he came to the door and I thought it was trick or treat, but it turned out he wanted Mark to come out with him. Just around the block, he said, because he didn't want to go alone. I told Mark no, he wasn't supposed to, and he had all the candy he wanted right here at home that you left for him. Besides, he didn't even have a costume. But Bill said it would only be for a few minutes, and Mark was almost crying, he wanted to go so bad. So I figured why not let him just as long as he promised to come right back and not go off the block? Besides, I told my boyfriend where I was sitting tonight and he called on the phone right in the middle of all this going on, so—"

"You mean you disobeyed our orders?" There was no slur in Irene's voice now, only the sharp shrill of sudden anger. "You let him go?"

"I'm sorry. I guess I wasn't thinking—"

"Never mind that." Howard's hoarse voice held apprehension as well as anger. "How long ago was this?"

"How long?" Connie shook her head. "I don't know. I mean, I was on the phone and then I started playing the stereo, like maybe around ten o'clock."

"Then he's been gone over an hour." Howard's face was grim. "Maybe an hour and a half, while you sat there blabbing with your boyfriend and listening to that goddamn rock crap!"

Connie began to cry, but Irene ignored her. She turned to her husband. "Why don't you get in the car and take a run around the block? He can't have gone very far."

"I hope to God you're right." Howard moved toward the hall. "Meanwhile, you better phone the Summerses and see if Bill brought him back over there."

"Good idea. I never thought of that." Irene was already dialing as Howard started up the car outside, and she could hear it pulling away as Mrs. Summers responded to her call.

"Hello—Midge?" Irene spoke quickly. "Sorry to bother you at this late hour, but I was wondering—"

Connie stood beside her, trying to control her sniffles as she listened. But Irene's words and the pauses between them told their own story, and when at last she hung up and turned her anguished face to the light Connie started to cry again.

"You heard?" Irene said. "Bill's gone too." Then her voice broke. "Oh my God!" She rose. "What's keeping Howard so long?"

The answer came as a car screeched to a halt in the driveway and Irene opened the front door to admit her husband. The night wind was cold, but what really chilled her as he entered was the realization that Howard was alone.

"No sign of him," he muttered. "I covered everything for a half mile up and down, and there's not a kid out anywhere."

"There wouldn't be, at this hour." Irene nodded. "I know he's not at the Summerses, but maybe he and Bill stopped by somewhere else. I'm going to phone the Coopers and see—"

"Don't bother," Howard said. "I've just come from there. And before that I looked in on the Stuttmans and those new people, Higgins or whatever their name is. Their kids haven't come home either."

"But that's impossible! Do you realize it's past eleven-thirty?" She trembled, fighting the tears. "Where could they be?"

"We'll find out." Howard brushed past her, striding toward the phone. "I'm calling the police."

The grandfather's clock began to boom its message of midnight as potbellied Benjamin Franklin and little old Mrs. See peered into the parlor at the left of the front hallway.

"I'm glad we used candy this time," she said. "And that was a good idea of yours, giving money instead if the youngsters came to the door with their parents."

It was dark in the parlor and they had only a moment to stare through the shadows at the huddled forms lying motionless within.

"How many are there?" he said.

"Thirteen." She beamed at him as the chimes came to an end. "At least we won't be going hungry."

Sergeant Lichner kept his cool, but it wasn't easy. The station was like a madhouse, all those parents yelling and crying, and it took a team of four men just to question them and get some facts, instead of listening to wild guesses about kidnappers or crazies who put razor blades in Halloween candy.

But in the end he got it all together, using the statements to map out a route. Putting through some phone calls to establish where each child or group of children had last been seen, it turned out that everything must have happened somewhere within the area of one square block.

Then he called in backups and started out. There were four black-and-whites assigned to the search, each with its quota of parents, and each taking a single side of the block as they went from door to door asking questions.

On three sides the answers formed a pattern. Various youngsters had knocked on doors at various times, but all had been seen and accounted for.

Sergeant Lichner himself was in a fifth car, and to speed matters up he took one end of the block while the fourth car started at the other.

It wasn't until the two cars converged in the middle of the block to compare notes that he got an answer. Sid Olney pulled up and got out, shaking his head. "They were here, all right," he said. "Stopped at every house back there, right on up until around eleven. What did you find out, anything?"

Sergeant Lichner took a deep breath. "Same as you." He glanced at the house directly behind him. "Folks in the last place said the Esterhazy kid and the Summers boy were there late, almost eleven-thirty. What time did your people see them?"

Sid Olney shook his head. "They didn't." He shook his head. "That's funny."

But there was no mirth in his eyes or the eyes of the parents as they stared at the spot where the trail ended—the space between the two houses looming on either side of the weed-choked vacant lot lying empty and deserted under the Halloween moon.

Everybody Needs a Little Love

It started out as a gag.

I'm sitting at the bar minding my own business, which was drinking up a storm, when this guy got to talking with me.

Curtis his name was, David Curtis. Big, husky-looking straight-arrow type; I figured him to be around thirty, same as me. He was belting it pretty good himself, so right off we had something in common. Curtis told me he was assistant manager of a department store, and since I'm running a video-game arcade in the same shopping mall we were practically neighbors. But talk about coincidence; turns out he'd just gotten a divorce three months ago, exactly like me.

Which is why we both ended up in the bar every night after work, at happy hour time. Two drinks for the price of one isn't a bad deal, not if you're trying to cut it with what's left after those monthly alimony payments.

"You think you got zapped?" Curtis said. "My ex-wife wiped me out. I'm not stuck for alimony, but I lost the house, the furniture, and the car. Then she hit me for the legal fees and I wind up with zero."

"I read you," I told him. "Gets to the point where you want out so bad you figure it's worth anything. But like the old saying, sometimes the cure is worse than the disease."

"This is my cure," Curtis said, finishing his scotch and ordering another round. "Trouble is, it doesn't work."

"So why are you here?" I asked. "You ought to try that singles bar down the street. Plenty of action there."

"Not for me." Curtis shook his head. "That's where I met my ex. Last thing I need is a singles bar."

"Me neither," I said. "But sometimes it's pretty lonesome just sitting around the apartment watching the late show. And I'm not into cooking or housework."

"I can handle that." Curtis rattled his rocks and the bartender poured a refill. "What gets me is going out. Ever notice what happens when you go to a restaurant by yourself? Even if the joint is empty they'll always steer you to one of those crummy little deuce tables in back, next to the kitchen or the men's john. The waiter gives you a dirty look because a loner means a smaller tip. And when the crowd starts coming in you can kiss service goodbye. The waiter forgets about your order, and when it finally comes, everything's cold. Then, after you finish, you sit around till hell freezes, waiting for your check."

"Right on," I said. "So maybe you need a change of pace."

"Like what?"

"Like taking a run up to Vegas some weekend. There's always ads in the paper for bargain rates on air fare and rooms."

"And every damned one of them is for couples." Curtis thumped his glass down on the bar. "Two for one on the plane tickets. Double occupancy for the rooms."

"Try escort service," I told him. "Hire yourself a date, no strings—"

"Not on my income. And I don't want to spend an evening or a weekend with some yacky broad trying to make small talk. What I need is the silent type."

"Maybe you could run an ad for a deaf mute?"

"Knock it off! This thing really bugs me. I'm tired of being treated like a cross between a leper and the Invisible Man."

"So what's the answer?" I said. "There's got to be a way—"

"Damn betcha!" Curtis stood up fast, which was a pretty good trick, considering the load he was carrying.

"Where you going?" I asked.

"Come along and see," he said.

Five minutes later I'm watching Curtis use his night key to unlock the back door of the department store.

Ten minutes later he has me sneaking around outside a storeroom in the dark, keeping an eye out for the security guard.

Fifteen minutes later I'm helping Curtis load a window dummy into the backseat of his rental car.

Like I said, it started out as a gag.

At least that's what I thought it was when he stole Estelle.

"That's her name," he told me. "Estelle."

This was a week later, the night he invited me over to his place for dinner. I stopped by the bar for a few quickies beforehand and when I got to his apartment I was feeling no pain. Even so, I started to get uptight the minute I walked in.

Seeing the window dummy sitting at the dinette table gave me a jolt, but when he introduced her by name it really rattled my cage.

"Isn't she pretty?" Curtis said.

I couldn't fault him on that. The dummy was something special: blond wig, baby blue eyes, long lashes, and a face with a kind of what-are-you-waiting-for smile. The arms and legs were what you call articulated, and her figure was the kind you see in centerfolds. On top of that, Curtis had dressed it up in an evening gown, with plenty of cleavage.

When he noticed me eyeballing the outfit he went over to a wall closet and slid the door open. Damned if he didn't have the rack full of women's clothes—suits, dresses, sports outfits, even a couple of nighties.

"From the store?" I asked.

Curtis nodded. "They'll never miss them until inventory, and I got tired of seeing her in the same old thing all the time. Besides, Estelle likes nice clothes."

I had to hand it to him, putting me on like this without cracking a smile.

"Sit down and keep her company," Curtis said. "I'll have dinner on the table in a minute."

I sat down. I mean, what the hell else was I going to do? But it gave me an antsy feeling to have a window dummy staring at me across the table in the candlelight. That's right, he'd put candles on the table, and in the shadows you had to look twice to make sure this was only a manikin or whatever you call it.

Curtis served up a couple of really good steaks and a nice tossed salad. He'd skipped the drinks-before-dinner routine; instead he poured a pretty fair Cabernet with the meal, raising his glass in a toast.

"To Estelle," he said.

I raised my glass too, feeling like a wimp but trying to go along with the gag. "How come she's not drinking?" I asked.

"Estelle doesn't drink." He still didn't smile. "That's one of the things I like about her."

It was the way he said it that got to me. I had to break up that straight face of his, so I gave him a grin. "I notice she isn't eating very much either."

Curtis nodded. "Estelle doesn't believe in stuffing her face. She wants to keep her figure."

He was still deadpanning, so I said, "If she doesn't drink and she doesn't eat, what happens when you take her to a restaurant?"

"We only went out once," Curtis told me. "Tell the truth, it wasn't the way I expected. They gave us a good table all right, but the waiter kept staring at us and the other customers started making wise-ass remarks under their breath, so now we eat at home. Estelle doesn't need restaurants."

The straighter he played it the more it burned me, so I gave it another shot. "Then I guess you won't be taking her to Vegas after all?"

"We went there last weekend," Curtis said. "I was right about the plane fare. Not only did I save a bundle but we got the red-carpet treatment. When they saw me carrying Estelle they must have figured her for an invalid: we got to board first and had our choice of seats up front. The stewardess even brought her a blanket."

Curtis was really on a roll now, and all I could do was go with it. "How'd you make out with the hotel?" I asked.

"No sweat. Double-occupancy rate, just like the ads said, plus complimentary cocktails and twenty dollars in free chips for the casino."

I tried one more time. "Did Estelle win any money?"

"Oh no—she doesn't gamble." Curtis shook his head. "We ended up spending the whole weekend right there in our room, phoning room service for meals and watching closed-circuit TV. Most of the time we never even got out of bed."

That shook me. "You were in bed with her?"

"Don't worry, it was king-size, plenty of room. And I found out another nice thing about Estelle. She doesn't snore."

I squeezed off another grin. "Then just what does she do when you go to bed with her?"

"Sleep, of course." Curtis did a double take. "Don't go getting any ideas. If I wanted the other thing I could have picked up one of those inflatable rubber floozies from a sex shop. But there's no hanky-panky with Estelle. She's a real lady."

"A real lady," I said. "Now I've heard everything."

"Not from her." Curtis nodded at the dummy. "Haven't you noticed? I've been doing all the talking and she hasn't said a word. You don't know how great it is to have someone around who believes in keeping her mouth shut. Sure, I do the cooking and the housework, but it's no more of a hassle than when I was living here alone."

"You don't feel alone anymore, is that it?"

"How could I? Now when I come home nights I've got some-body waiting for me. No nagging, no curlers in the hair—just the way she is now, neat and clean and well dressed. She even uses that perfume I gave her. Can't you smell it?"

Damned if he wasn't right. I *could* smell perfume.

I sneaked another peek at Estelle. Sitting in the shadows with the candlelight soft on her hair and face, she almost had me fooled for a minute. Almost, but not quite.

"Just look at her," Curtis said. "Beautiful! Look at that smile!"

Now, for the first time, he smiled too. And it was his smile I looked at, not hers.

"Okay," I said. "You win. If you're trying to tell me Estelle is better company than most women, it's no contest."

"I figured you'd understand." Curtis hadn't changed his expression, but there was something wrong about that smile of his, something that got to me.

So I had to say it. "I don't want to be a party pooper, but the way you come on, maybe there's such a thing as carrying a gag too far."

He wasn't smiling now. "Who said anything about a gag? Are you trying to insult Estelle?"

"I'm not trying to insult anybody," I told him. "Just remember, she's only a dummy."

"Dummy?" All of a sudden he was on his feet and coming

around the table, waving those big fists of his. "You're the one who's a dummy! Get the hell out of here before I—"

I got out, before.

Then I went over to the bar, had three fast doubles, and headed for home to hit the sack. I went out like a light but it didn't keep the dreams away, and all night long I kept staring at the smiles—the smile on his face and the smile on the dummy's—and I don't know which one spooked me the most.

Come to think of it, they both looked the same.

That night was the last I went to the bar for a long time. I didn't want to run into Curtis there, but I was still seeing him in those dreams.

I did my drinking at home now, but the dreams kept coming, and it loused me up at work when I was hung over. Pretty soon I started pouring a shot at breakfast instead of orange juice.

So I went to see Dr. Mannerheim.

That shows how rough things were getting, because I don't like doctors and I've always had a thing about shrinks. This business of lying on a couch and spilling your guts to a stranger always bugged me. But it got to where I started calling in sick and just sat home staring at the walls. Next thing you knew I'd start climbing them.

I told Mannerheim that when I saw him.

"Don't worry," he said. "I won't ask you to lie on a couch or take inkblot tests. The physical shows you're a little rundown, but this can be corrected by proper diet and a vitamin supplement. Chances are you may not even need therapy at all."

"Then what am I here for?" I said.

"Because you have a problem. Suppose we talk about it."

Dr. Mannerheim was just a little bald-headed guy with glasses; he looked a lot like an uncle of mine who used to take me to ball games when I was a kid. So it wasn't as hard to talk as I'd expected.

I filled him in on my setup—the divorce and all—and he picked up on it right away. Said it was getting to be a common thing nowadays with so many couples splitting. There's always a hassle working out a new life-style afterward and sometimes a kind of guilty feeling; you keep wondering if it was your fault and that maybe something's wrong with you.

We got into the sex bit and the drinking, and then he asked me about my dreams.

That's when I told him about Curtis.

Before I knew it I'd laid out the whole thing—getting smashed in the bar, stealing the dummy, going to Curtis's place for dinner, and what happened there.

"Just exactly what did happen?" Mannerheim said. "You say you had a few drinks before you went to his apartment—maybe three or four—and you drank wine with your dinner."

"I wasn't bombed, if that's what you mean."

"But your perceptions were dulled," he told me. "Perhaps he intended to put you on for a few laughs, but when he saw your condition he got carried away."

"If you'd seen the way he looked when he told me to get out you'd know it wasn't a gag," I said. "The guy is a nut case."

Something else hit me all of a sudden, and I sat up straight in my chair. "I remember a movie I saw once. There's this ventriloquist who gets to thinking his dummy is alive. Pretty soon he starts talking to it, then he gets jealous of it, and next thing you know—"

Mannerheim held up his hand. "Spare me the details. There must be a dozen films like that. But in all my years of practice I've never read of, let alone run across, a single case where such a situation actually existed. It all goes back to the old Greek legend about Pygmalion, the sculptor who made a statue of a beautiful woman that came to life.

"But you've got to face facts." He ticked them off on his fingers. "Your friend Curtis has a manikin, not a ventriloquist's dummy. He doesn't try to create the illusion that it speaks, or use his hand to make it move. And he didn't create the figure, he's not a sculptor. So what does that leave us with?"

"Just one thing," I said. "He's treating this dummy like a real person."

Mannerheim shook his head. "A man who's capable of carrying a window dummy into a restaurant and a hotel—or who claims to have done so in order to impress you—may still just have taken advantage of your condition to play out an elaborate practical joke."

"Wrong." I stood up. "I tell you he believes the dummy is alive."

"Maybe and maybe not. It isn't important." Mannerheim took off his glasses and stared at me. "What's important is that *you* believe the dummy is alive."

It hit me like a sock in the gut. I had to sit down again and catch my breath before I could answer him.

"You're right," I said. "That's why I really wanted out of there. That's why I keep having those damned dreams. That's why there's a drinking problem. Maybe I was juiced up when I saw her, maybe Curtis hypnotized me, how the hell do I know? But whatever happened or didn't happen, it worked. And I've been running scared ever since."

"Then stop running." Dr. Mannerheim put his glasses on again. "The only way to fight fear is to face it."

"You mean go back there?"

He nodded at me. "If you want to get rid of the dreams, get rid of the dependency on alcohol, the first step is to separate fantasy from reality. Go to Curtis, and go sober. Examine the actual circumstances with a clear head. I'm satisfied that you'll see things differently. Then, if you still think you need further help, get in touch."

We both stood up, and Dr. Mannerheim walked me to the door. "Have a good day," he said.

I didn't.

It took all that weekend just to go over what he'd said, and another two days before I could buy his advice. But it made sense. Maybe Curtis had been setting me up like the shrink said; if not, then he was definitely a flake. But one way or another I had to find out.

So Wednesday night I went up to the apartment. I wasn't on the sauce, and I didn't call Curtis in advance. That way, if he didn't know I was coming, he wouldn't plan on pulling another rib—if it was a rib.

It must have been close to nine o'clock when I walked down

the hall and knocked on his door. There was no answer; maybe he was gone for the evening. But I kept banging away, just in case, and finally the door opened.

"Come on in," Curtis said.

I stared at him. He was wearing a pair of dirty, wrinkled-up pajamas, but he looked like he hadn't slept for a week: his face was gray, big circles under his eyes, and he needed a shave. When we shook hands I felt like I was holding a sack of ice cubes.

"Good to see you," he told me, closing the door after I got inside. "I was hoping you'd come by so's I could apologize for the way I acted the other night."

"No hard feelings," I said.

"I knew you wouldn't hold it against me," he went on. "That's what I told Estelle."

Curtis turned and nodded across the living room, and in the dim light I saw the dummy sitting there on the sofa, facing the TV screen. The set was turned on to some old Western movie, but the sound was way down and I could scarcely hear the dialogue.

It didn't matter, because I was looking at the dummy. She wore some kind of fancy cocktail dress, which figured, because I could see the bottle on the coffee table and smell the whiskey on Curtis's breath. What grabbed me was the other stuff she was wearing— the earrings, and the bracelet with the big stones that sparkled and gleamed. They had to be costume jewelry, but they looked real in the light from the TV tube. And the way the dummy sat, sort of leaning forward, you'd swear it was watching the screen.

Only I knew better. Seeing the dummy cold sober this way, it was just a wooden figure, like the others I saw in the storeroom where Curtis stole it. Dr. Mannerheim was right; now that I got a good look the dummy didn't spook me anymore.

Curtis went over to the coffee table and picked up the bottle. "Care for a drink?" he asked.

I shook my head. "No, thanks, not now."

But he kept on holding the bottle when he bent down and kissed the dummy on the side of its head. "How can you hear anything with the sound so low?" he said. "Let me turn up the volume for you."

And so help me, that's what he did. Then he smiled at the

dummy. "I don't want to interrupt while you're watching, honey. So if it's okay with you, we'll go in the bedroom and talk there."

He moved back across the living room and started down the hall. I followed him into the bedroom at the far end and he closed the door. It shut off the sound from the TV set but now I heard another noise, a kind of chirping.

Looking over at the far corner I saw the birdcage on a stand, with a canary hopping around inside.

"Estelle likes canaries," Curtis said. "Same as my ex. She always had a thing for pets." He tilted the bottle.

I just stood there staring at the room. It was a real disaster area—bed not made, heaped-up clothes lying on the floor, empty fifths and glasses everywhere. The place smelled like a zoo.

The bottle stopped gurgling and then I heard the whisper. "Thank God you came."

I glanced up at Curtis. He wasn't smiling now. "You've got to help me," he said.

"What's the problem?" I asked.

"Keep your voice down," he whispered. "I don't want her to hear us."

"Don't start that again," I told him. "I only stopped in because I figured you'd be straightened out by now."

"How can I? She doesn't let me out of her sight for a minute; the last time I got away from here was three days ago, when I turned in the rental car and bought her the Mercedes."

That threw me. "Mercedes? You're putting me on."

Curtis shook his head. "It's downstairs in the garage right now—brand-new 280-SL, hasn't been driven since I brought it home. Estelle doesn't like me to go out alone and she doesn't want to go out either. I keep hoping she'll change her mind because I'm sick of being cooped up here, eating those frozen TV dinners. You'd think she'd at least go for a drive with me after getting her the car and all."

"I thought you told me you were broke," I said. "Where'd you get the money for a Mercedes?"

He wouldn't look at me. "Never mind. That's my business."

"What about your business?" I asked. "How come you haven't been showing up at work?"

"I quit my job," he whispered. "Estelle told me to."

"Told you? Make sense, man. Window dummies don't talk."

He gave me a glassy-eyed stare. "Who said anything about window dummies? Don't you remember how it was the night we got her—how she was standing there in the storage room waiting for me? The others were dummies all right, I know that. But Estelle knew I was coming, so she just stood there pretending to be like all the rest because she didn't want you to catch on.

"She fooled you, right? I'm the only one who knew Estelle was different. There were all kinds of dummies there, some real beauties, too. But the minute I laid eyes on her I knew she was the one.

"And it was great, those first few days with her. You saw for yourself how well we got along. It wasn't until afterward that everything went wrong, when she started telling me about all the stuff she wanted, giving me orders, making me do crazy things."

"Look," I said. "If there's anything crazy going on around here, you're the one who's responsible. And you better get your act together and put a stop to it right now. Maybe you can't do it alone, the shape you're in, but I've got a friend, a doctor—"

"Doctor? You think I'm whacko, is that it?" He started shaking all over and there was a funny look in his eyes. "Here I thought you'd help me, you were my last hope!"

"I want to help," I told him. "That's why I came. First off, let's try to clean this place up. Then you're going to bed, get a good night's rest."

"What about Estelle?" he whispered.

"Leave that to me. When you wake up tomorrow I promise the dummy'll be gone."

That's when he threw the bottle at my head.

I was still shaking the next afternoon when I got to Dr. Mannerheim's office and told him what happened.

"Missed me by inches," I said. "But it sure gave me one hell of a scare. I ran down the hall to the living room. The damn dummy was still sitting in front of the TV like it was listening to the program and that scared me too, all over again. I kept right on running until I got home. That's when I called your answering service."

Mannerheim nodded at me. "Sorry it took so long to get back to you. I had some unexpected business."

"Look, Doc," I said. "I've been thinking. Curtis wasn't really trying to hurt me. The poor guy's so uptight he doesn't realize what he's doing anymore. Maybe I should have stuck around, tried to calm him down."

"You did the right thing." Mannerheim took off his glasses and polished them with his handkerchief. "Curtis is definitely psychotic, and very probably dangerous."

That shook me. "But when I came here last week you said he was harmless—"

Dr. Mannerheim put his glasses on. "I know. But since then I've found out a few things."

"Like what?"

"Your friend Curtis lied when he told you he quit his job. He didn't quit; he was fired."

"How do you know?"

"I heard about it the day after I saw you, when his boss called me in. I was asked to run a series of tests on key personnel as part of a security investigation. It seems that daily bank deposits for the store show a fifty-thousand-dollar loss in the cash flow. Somebody juggled the books."

"The Mercedes!" I said. "So that's where he got the money!"

"We can't be sure just yet. But polygraph tests definitely rule out other employees who had access to the records. We do know where he bought the car. The dealer only got a down payment so the rest of the cash, around forty thousand, is still unaccounted for."

"Then it's all a scam, right, Doc? What he really means to do is take the cash and split out. He was running a number on me about the dummy, trying to make me think he's bananas, so I wouldn't tumble to what he's up to."

"I'm afraid it isn't that simple." Mannerheim got up and started pacing the floor. "I've been doing some rethinking about Curtis and his hallucination that the dummy is alive. That canary you mentioned; a pity he didn't get it before he stole the manikin."

"What are you driving at?"

"There are a lot of lonely people in this world, people who

aren't necessarily lonely by choice. Some are elderly, some have lost all close relatives through death, some suffer an aftershock following divorce. But all of them have one thing in common: the need for love. Not physical love, necessarily, but what goes with it. The companionship, attention, a feeling of mutual affection. That's why so many of them turn to keeping pets.

"I'm sure you've seen examples. The man who spends all his time taking care of his dog. The widow who babies her kitten. The old lady who talks to her canary, treating it like an equal."

I nodded. "The way Curtis treats the dummy?"

Mannerheim settled down in his chair again. "Usually they don't go that far. But in extreme cases the pretense gets out of hand. They not only talk to their pets, they interpret each growl or purr or chirp as a reply. It's called personification."

"But these pet owners—they're harmless, aren't they? So why do you say Curtis might be dangerous?"

Dr. Mannerheim leaned forward in his chair. "After talking to the people at the store I did a little further investigation on my own. This morning I went down to the courthouse and checked the files. Curtis told you he got a divorce here in town three months ago, but there's no record of any proceedings. And I found out he was lying to you about other things. He was married, all right; he did own a house and furniture and a car. But there's nothing to show he ever turned anything over to his wife. Chances are he sold his belongings to pay off gambling debts. We know he did some heavy betting at the track."

"We?" I said. "You and who else?"

"Sheriff's department. They're the ones who told me about his wife's disappearance, three months ago."

"You mean she ran out on him?"

"That's what he said after neighbors noticed she was missing and they called him in. He told them downtown that he'd come home from work one night and his wife was gone, bag and baggage—no explanation, no note, nothing. He denied they'd quarreled, said he'd been too ashamed to report her absence, and had kept hoping she'd come back or at least get in touch with him."

"Did they buy his story?"

Mannerheim shrugged. "Women do leave their husbands,

for a variety of reasons, and there was nothing to show Curtis wasn't telling the truth. They put out an all-points on his wife and kept the file open. But so far no new information has turned up, not until this embezzlement matter and your testimony. I didn't mention that this morning, but I have another appointment this evening and I'll tell them then. I think they'll take action, once they hear your evidence."

"Wait a minute," I said. "I haven't given you any evidence."

"I think you have." Mannerheim stared at me. "According to the neighbors, Curtis was married to a tall blonde with blue eyes, just like the window dummy you saw. And his wife's name was Estelle."

It was almost dark by the time I got to the bar. The happy hour had started, but I wasn't happy. All I wanted was a drink—a couple of drinks—enough to make me forget the whole thing.

Only it didn't work out that way. I kept thinking about what Mannerheim told me, about Curtis and the mess he was in.

The guy was definitely psyched out, no doubt about that. He'd ripped off his boss, lost his job, screwed up his life.

But maybe it wasn't his fault. I knew what he'd gone through because I'd been there myself. Getting hit with a divorce was bad enough to make me slip my gears, and for him it must have been ten times worse. Coming home and finding his wife gone, just like that, without a word. He never said so, but he must have loved her—loved her so much that when she left him he flipped out, stealing the dummy, calling it by her name. Even when he got to feeling trapped he couldn't give the dummy up because it reminded him of his wife. All this was pretty far out, but I could understand. Like Mannerheim said, everybody needs a little love.

If anyone was to blame, it was that wife of his. Maybe she split because she was cheating on him, the way mine did. The only difference is that I could handle it and he cracked up. Now he'd either be tossed in the slammer or get put away in a puzzle factory, and all because of love. His scuzzy wife got away free and he got dumped on. After Mannerheim talked to the law they'd probably come and pick him up tonight; poor guy, he didn't have a chance.

Unless I gave it to him.

I ordered up another drink and thought about that. Sure, if I tipped him off and told him to run it could get me into a bind. But who would know? The thing of it was, I could understand Curtis, even put myself in his place. Both of us had the same raw deal, but I'd lucked out and he couldn't take it. Maybe I owed him something—at least a lousy phone call.

So I went over to the pay phone at the end of the bar. This big fat broad was using the phone, probably somebody's cheating wife handing her husband a line about why she wasn't home. When I came up she gave me a dirty look and kept right on yapping.

It was getting on toward eight o'clock now. I didn't know when Dr. Mannerheim's appointment was set with the sheriff's department, but there wouldn't be much time left. And Curtis's apartment was only three blocks away.

I made it in five minutes, walking fast. So fast that I didn't even look around when I crossed in front of the entrance to the building's underground parking place.

If I hadn't heard the horn I'd have been a goner. As it was, there were just about two seconds for me to jump back when the big blue car came tearing up the ramp and wheeled into the street. Just two seconds to get out of the way, look up, and see the Mercedes take off.

Then I took off too, running into the building and down the hall.

The only break I got was finding Curtis's apartment door wide open. He was gone—I already knew that—but all I wanted now was to use the phone.

I called the sheriff's office and Dr. Mannerheim was there. I told him where I was and about seeing the car take off, and after that things happened fast.

In a couple of minutes a full squad of deputies wheeled in. They went through the place and came up with zilch. No Curtis, no Estelle; even the dummy's clothes were missing. And if he had forty grand or so stashed away, that was gone too; all they found was a rip in a sofa cushion where he could have hidden the loot.

But another squad had better luck, if you can call it that. They located the blue Mercedes in an old gravel pit off the highway about five miles out of town.

Curtis was lying on the ground next to it, stone-cold dead, with a big butcher knife stuck between his shoulder blades. The dummy was there too, lying a few feet away. The missing money was in Curtis's wallet—all big bills—and the dummy's wardrobe was in the rear seat, along with Curtis's luggage, like he'd planned to cut out of town for good.

Dr. Mannerheim was with the squad out there and he was the one who suggested digging into the pit. It sounded wild, but he kept after them until they moved a lot of gravel. His hunch paid off, because about six feet down they hit pay dirt. It was a woman's body, or what was left of it after three months in the ground.

The coroner's office had a hell of a time making an I.D. It turned out to be Curtis's wife, of course, and there were about twenty stab wounds on her, all made with a butcher knife like the one that killed Curtis.

Funny thing, they couldn't get any prints off the handle, but there were a lot of funny things about the whole business. Dr. Mannerheim figured Curtis killed his wife and buried her in the pit, and what sent him over the edge was guilt feelings. So he stole the dummy and tried to pretend it was his wife. Calling her Estelle, buying all those things for her, he was trying to make up for what he'd done, and finally he got to the point where he really thought she was alive.

Maybe that makes sense, but it still doesn't explain how Curtis was killed, or why.

I could ask some other questions too. If you really believe something with all your heart and soul, how long does it take before it comes true? And how long does a murder victim lie in her grave plotting to get even?

But I'm not going to say anything. If I told them my reasons they'd say I was crazy too.

All I know is that when the Mercedes came roaring out of the garage I only had two seconds to get out of the way. But it was long enough for me to get a good look, long enough for me to swear I saw Curtis and the dummy together in the front seat.

And Estelle was the one behind the wheel.

The Totem Pole

Arthur Shurm belonged to the vast army of the unidentified—that mighty swarm of nonentities which includes streetcar conductors, restaurant countermen, elevator operators, bellboys, theater ushers, and other public servants wearing uniforms of their professions. One never seems to notice their faces; their garb is a designation of official capacity, and the body within makes no impression on the memory.

Arthur Shurm was one of those men. To be exact, he was a museum attendant, and surely there is no employment which makes a person less conspicuous. One might perchance take notice of a counterman's voice when he bellows "Two sunny side up and cuppa cawfee"; it is possible to observe the demeanor of a bellboy as he lingers for a tip; one can perhaps mark the particularly erect subservience of an individual usher as he leads his party down the aisle. But a museum attendant never speaks, it seems. There is nothing about his carriage or manner to impress a visitor. Then too, his personality is totally overshadowed by the background in which he moves—the vast palace of death and decay which is a museum. Of all the unidentified army, the museum attendant is beyond doubt the most self-effacing.

And yet the fact remains that I shall never forget Arthur Shurm. I wish to heaven I could.

I

I was standing in the tavern at the bar. Never mind what I was doing there; let's say I was looking for local color. The truth is, I was waiting for a girl and had been stood up. It happens to everybody. At any rate, I was standing there when Arthur Shurm rushed in. I stared at him.

It was the natural thing to do. A museum attendant is a museum attendant, after all. He is a little man in a blue uniform—a quite nondescript blue uniform, lacking the gaudiness of a policeman's outfit, or the dignified buttons that adorn a fireman. A museum attendant wears his inconspicuous garb, standing stolidly in the shadows before mummy cases or geological specimens. He may be old or young; one simply never notices him. He always moves slowly, quietly, with an air of abstract deliberation which seems part and parcel of the museum's background, its total disregard of time.

So it was natural for me to turn and stare at Arthur Shurm when he ran into the tavern. I had never seen such movement before.

There were other arresting things, however, which emphasized his entrance. The way his pale face twitched, for example; the roll of his bloodshot eyes—these were phenomena impossible to overlook. And his hoarse voice, gasping for a drink, quite electrified me.

The bartender, urbane as all such servitors of Bacchus, never flickered an eyelash as he poured the whiskey. Arthur Shurm gulped down his drink, and the look in his eyes made it unnecessary for him to ask for a second one. It was poured, and as quickly downed. Then Arthur Shurm put his head down on the bar and began to cry. The bartender blandly turned away. Nothing surprises a tavernkeeper. But I was the only other customer, and I edged down the rail and braced the weeping museum attendant on the shoulder.

"Come on, now," I said, signaling the acolyte of Silenus to refill our glasses. "What's up, man?"

Arthur Shurm gazed at me through tears, not of sorrow, but of agonized remembrance. I felt that gaze, pouring from bloodshot eyes that had seen too much. I knew that the man could never contain such memories within himself alone. The story was coming. And when Shurm had drunk the third drink, it came.

"Thanks. Thanks, I needed that. Guess I'm pretty upset. Sorry."

I smiled reassuringly at his incoherency. He braced himself.

"Look here, mister. Let me talk to you. Got to talk to someone. Then I'll go out and find a cop."

"Any trouble?"

"Yes—no—not what you think. It isn't the *right* kind of trouble. See what I mean? I have to talk to someone first. Then I'll get a cop."

I had the glasses refilled and led Shurm to a booth where the bartender could not overhear. Shurm sat there and trembled until I grew impatient.

"Now then," I said, briskly. The firmness in my voice was just what he had been looking for. He needed such reassurance of strength. He was almost eager to talk.

"I'll tell it to you straight. Straight, like it was a story or something. Then you can judge making heads or tails out of it all. I'll tell it to you from the beginning and leave it up to you, mister."

Lord, he *was* frightened!

"My name's Arthur Shurm. I'm caretaker over at the Public Museum up the street. You know it. Been there six years and never had any trouble. Ask anybody once if I ever had trouble. I'm not crazy, mister. They thought I was this week, but I'm not. After tonight I can prove I'm O.K.—but something else is crazy. That's what gets me. Something else is crazy, and that nearly drives me nuts."

I waited. Shurm rattled on.

"Like I say, here it is from the beginning. I been six years on the second floor—American Indian ethnology. Room 12. It was fine until last week. That's when they brought in the totem pole. *The totem pole!*"

He had no reason to scream, and I told him so.

"Sorry. I have to tell you about the pole, though. Shoshoonack Indian totem pole, from Alaska. Dr. Bailey brought it back last week. He was up there on an expedition someplace in the mountains, where these Shoshoonack Indians live. They're a new tribe or something; don't know much about them. So Dr. Bailey he went up there with Dr. Fiske to get a few things for the museum. And last week Dr. Bailey came back home with the totem pole. Dr. Fiske died up there. He died there, don't you see?"

I didn't see, but I ordered another drink.

"That totem pole he brought back—he had it set up in the

American Indian room right away. It was a new pole, carved especially for him by the medicine men of the tribe. About ten feet tall it was, with faces all over it; you know how they look. Horrible thing.

"But Bailey was proud of it. He was proud of all he had done up there in the Shoshoonack country, bringing back a mess of pottery and picture-writings and stuff that was new to the curators and the big professors. He had them all in to look at it, and I guess he wrote up an article on the customs of the Shoshoonacks for some official report. Bailey is that kind of a man, very proud; I always hated him. Fat, greasy fellow, used to bawl me out for not dusting around proper. Crazy about his work, though.

"Anyhow, Bailey was awfully set up over his discoveries, and he didn't even seem to be sorry about Dr. Fiske dying there in Alaska. Seems Fiske had some kind of fever and just kicked off in a few days. Bailey never even talked about it, but I know for a fact that Fiske did most of the work. You see, he was the one who found out about the Shoshoonack Indians in the first place, and he ran the expedition. Bailey had just come along, and now he strutted around claiming all the credit. He used to bring in visitors to see that ugly totem pole and tell how it was made specially for him by the grateful Indians and presented to him just before he left for home. Oh, he was cocky enough!

"I'll never forget the day we first put in the totem pole and I got a good look at the thing. I'm used enough to outlandish stuff on the job, mister, but one look at this totem pole was enough. It gave me the creeps.

"You've seen them? Well, never one like this. You know what they mean—symbols of the tribe, sort of a coat of arms; made up of faces of bear-gods and beavers and owl-spirits, one on top of the other? This totem pole was different. It was just faces; six human faces one on top of the other, with arms sticking out at the sides. And those faces were awful. Big staring red eyes, and grinning yellow teeth like fangs; all snarling brown faces leering out in a row so that they seemed to be looking right at you all the time. When the shadows hit the pole about midafternoon you could still see the eyes sort of glowing in the dark. Gave me a fright that first time, I tell you.

"But Dr. Bailey came in, fat and snappy in a new suit, and he brought a raft of professors and big shots, and they stood around examining the pole while Bailey jabbered like a monkey who just found a new coconut. He dragged out a magnifying glass and puttered with it, trying to identify the wood and the kind of paint used, and bragging how the medicine man, Shawgi, had it done as a special going-away present and made the men of the tribe work night and day to get it done.

"I hung around and listened. Things were kinda quiet anyway. Bailey was telling about the way they carved the thing in the medicine man's big hut working only at night, with seven fires set around the place so no one could get in. They burned herbs in the fires to call down the spirits, and all the time they worked the men in the hut prayed out loud in long chants. Bailey claimed that the totem poles were the most sacred things the Shoshoonacks had; they thought the spirits of their dead chiefs went into the poles, and every time a chief died a pole was made to set up in front of his family's hut. Shawgi, the medicine man, was supposed to summon the dead chief's spirit to inhabit the pole, and this called for a lot of chants and prayers.

"Oh, it was interesting stuff. Bailey laid it on and everybody was impressed. But none of them could figure out just how the pole had been put together, whether it was one piece of wood or a whole lot of pieces. They didn't find out what kind of wood it was, either, or the nature of the paint used to ornament those ugly-looking heads. One of the professors asked Bailey just what the faces on this pole meant, and Bailey admitted he didn't know; it was just a special job made by the medicine man to give to him as a farewell gift before he left. But all this set me figuring, and after the crowd went away, I had another look at the pole. I had a good look, too, because of something I noticed."

He paused. "This may sound long and silly to you now, mister, but I got good reason to tell you all this. I want to explain what I noticed about them faces. They weren't *artificial* enough. Do you know what I mean? Usually Indian carving is kinda stiff and square-cut. But these faces were done real carefully, and they were all different, just like they were sculptures of human heads. And the arms were carved out perfectly, with hands on the ends. That just don't seem natural. I didn't like it when I found this out—more so because it was getting dark already and those eyes gleamed at me there, just as though these were real heads that could see me. It was a queer thing to think, but that's the way I felt.

"And the next day I thought so more. I walked through the room all day and couldn't help taking a look every time I passed the totem pole. Seemed to me that the faces were getting *clearer*; I could recognize each one of the bottom four now, just like the faces of people I knew. The top ones were a little high up to see closely, and I didn't bother about those two. But the bottom four looked like human faces, now—evil, creepy faces. They grinned so, showing their teeth, and when I walked away I got the feeling that their red eyes were following me, just like people stare at your back.

"After about two days I got used to that, but then last Friday night I worked late cleaning, just as I did tonight. And last Friday night I *heard*.

"It was about nine o'clock and I was all alone in the building—all alone except for Bailey. He stays in his office generally to do work late. But I was the only one in the place; for sure the only one on the second floor. I was cleaning Room 11—the one just before the American Indian room, you know—when I heard voices.

"No, I wasn't puzzled, like a guy in a book. I didn't think of anything else, couldn't. Right away I thought *those Indians on the totem pole were talking.*

"Low, mumbling voices. Talking in whispers almost, or voices from very far away. Talking in gibberish I couldn't understand—Indian talk. I edged near the door, and I swear I don't know whether I meant to sneak in on them or run away. But I heard the voices just whisper alone in the dark room; not one, or two, or three voices, but all of them. Indian talk. And then a high voice—a different voice. It came so quick I didn't catch all, but I heard the word. 'Bailey,' it said, at the end. Then I thought I was crazy, and on top of that I was scared stiff. I ran down the hall and downstairs to the office and dragged Bailey back with me. Made him come quietly, without telling him a thing. We got to Room 11 and I just held him there while the droning talk went on.

"He was pale as a sheet. I snapped the lights on and we went in. Bailey kept staring at the totem pole. It was all right, of course, and there weren't any noises coming from it now. But it was all wrong in another way. Those faces were too easy for me to recognize now—those Indian faces. They stared at me and they stared at Bailey, and every second they seemed to snarl more and more. I couldn't keep looking at them, so I watched Bailey.

"Ever see a frightened fat man? Bailey was almost fainting. He kept looking and looking, and then his eyes seemed to go all black in the pupils and he began to mumble to himself. He did a funny thing. He looked at the bottom of the pole and then he pulled his head up real slowly, from one jerk to another. I knew he was watching each face in turn. And he mumbled.

"'Kowi, Umsa, Wipi, Sigatch, Molkwi,' he said. He said it three times, so I remember. He said it in five separate words, like he was calling off names. Then he began shaking and groaning. 'It's them,' he said. 'It's them all right. All five of them. But who's on top? All five of them that went over the cliff. But how could Shawgi know that? And what did he mean to do, giving me this? It's mad—but there they are. Kowi, Umsa, Wipi, Sigatch, Molkwi, and— Good God!'

"He ran out of the room like doom was at his heels. I turned out the lights quick and followed. I didn't wait around to see if the whispering started again, either, and I had enough of looking at those faces. I went out and had a few stiff drinks that night, I can tell you. Oh—thanks, mister. Thanks a lot. I can use this one with what I still got to tell you. I'll make it short, too. We have to get a cop.

"Well, Monday, Bailey got me before I went on duty. He looked plenty pale around the gills, and I could see he hadn't slept any better than I did. 'I think it's better if we forget about last Friday night, Shurm,' he said. 'Both of us were a little upset.'

"I wasn't that easy. 'What do you think is wrong, Doctor?' I asked him.

"He knew enough not to stall. 'I don't know,' he said. 'All I can say is that the faces on that totem pole are those of Indians I knew up in the Shoshoonack country—Indians that died in an accident, going over a cliff in a dogsled.' He looked sick when he said this.

'But don't say anything to anyone, Shurm. I give you my word I'm going to investigate this fully,' he says, 'and when I get the facts I'll let you know.'

"With that he slipped me five dollars.

"So I worked along, but I wasn't happy. I didn't go into that room any more than I had to on Monday or Tuesday, and still I just couldn't get ideas out of my head. Queer ideas. Ideas about how the medicine man, Shawgi, used to call souls to put in the totem poles he made. Ideas of how Dr. Bailey might be lying some way about this accident he claimed the Indians were killed in. Ideas of how Shawgi gave the totem pole to Bailey knowing it would haunt him. Ideas like that, and always the pictures of those terrible grinning faces and the little thin whispering in the dark.

"Wednesday I noticed Bailey go into the room. It was raining out, and the place was just about empty, and Bailey went into the room. He didn't know I'd seen him go in, and I was just curious enough to follow him, and mighty curious to stick behind a case and listen when I saw he was kneeling on the floor in front of the totem pole and praying.

"'Save me,' he mumbles. 'Spare me. I didn't know. I didn't mean to do it. I killed you—I cut the thongs on the harness and when the sled rounded the bend it went over. That I did. But you were present when I did—the other—I couldn't spare you as witnesses. I couldn't.'

"He sounded crazy, but I was guessing what he meant. He had killed those Indians, as I suspected, to hush them up about something else. And so Shawgi had fixed up the totem pole to haunt him with it.

"Then Bailey began talking real low, and I heard him say something about Dr. Fiske and the way he had died; how Shawgi had been Fiske's friend, and how Fiske and Bailey had quarreled. The truth came to me then. I knew that Bailey had killed Fiske, instead of Fiske dying of fever like he was supposed to. Probably they had gone on a trip after specimens with the Indians. Bailey had killed Fiske to steal his trophies and the credit of the expedition. The Indians had found out about it. So Bailey had tampered with the sled and sent the Indians over the cliff on the way back. Shawgi made the totem of their faces and gave it to Bailey to drive him crazy.

"Well, it looked as though he was succeeding. Bailey whimpered like a dog, crawling on the floor in front of those six grinning faces in the gloom, and it made me really sick to see it. I was going crazy too, hearing voices and looking at smiles from wooden faces. I got out without going back to that room.

"Thursday was my day off, and it pleased me. Today I went back. First one I saw was Bailey. He looked almost as though he was dying. 'What's the dope, Doctor?' I said.

"He just shook his head. Then he whispered. 'There were voices again last night, Shurm. And I could understand them.' I looked to see if he was kidding, but no. He bent down close. 'Voices came to me in the night. I wasn't here. I was home. But they came. They can come anywhere. I hear them now. They called me to the museum. They wanted me to come very much last night. All of them did—the *other*, too. I nearly went. Tell me, Shurm—for the mercy of God—did you hear voices too?'

"I shook my head.

" 'I'm going to take that totem pole down as soon as I can,' he went on. 'I'm going to take it down and have it burned. I will get permission today from the chief. He must let me. If not you and I shall have to tell him what we know. I'm relying on you. We must beat that devil Shawgi—he hated me, I know—that's why he did this—beating his drums and calling up devils with his magic while he carved the faces to hide the souls that wait—'

"Then someone came by, and Bailey went off.

"That afternoon I couldn't help myself; I went in and looked at the totem pole once again. Funny the way I trembled when I passed the door; it was getting me, too. Now that I had guessed about the murdered Indians I could see that the faces were taken from real life. I looked at them all—even the top one. The sixth one I still couldn't recognize; it might be the face of the medicine man, Shawgi, himself. But it was the worst of all the smiling wicked faces with white teeth through which they whispered at night. At night!

"Tonight I was going to have to stay and look over the place; clean up. I didn't want to. I had too much to think about. Would

I have to hear voices again? And downstairs working would be Bailey—the man I suspected of six murders. Yet I couldn't do a thing. No one would believe me, and I had no proof of either voices or Bailey being guilty. I worried, and all the time it got darker and darker, and the museum closed, and I began to go over the second floor room by room. Bailey was down in the office, working.

"About an hour and a half ago I was in Room 10. I heard the voices two rooms away. They were loud tonight; loud as if they were calling. I could hear grunting Indian sounds. And then I heard the high voice calling.

"'Bailey! Bailey! Come here, Bailey! I'm waiting, Bailey—I'm waiting!'

"I was scared sick when Bailey came, a minute later. He walked slow as if he didn't see me, and his eyes were all black pupil. In his hand he had a matchbox, and under his arm was a jug of kerosene. I knew what he was going to do.

"The voices were grumbling louder, but I had to follow. I didn't dare use any lights. Bailey went in ahead of me, and then I heard that laughing.

"It was the laughing that made me stop. I can't tell you about it, except that it was horrible—a chuckling laugh that went right through me. And someone—*something*—said 'Hello, Bailey.' Then I knew I was crazy, because I recognized the voice. For a minute I was stunned. Then I ran into the room.

"Just as I got near the doorway the screaming started. Bailey was screaming, and it mixed in with the awful laughing, and I heard a scrabbling sound and a crash as the kerosene jug fell. I pulled out my flashlight and I saw it. Lord!

"I didn't wait. I ran out. I came here. I want a cop. I haven't gone back yet. I want you to get the cop with me and come back. I want you should believe me and see what I saw. Oh—"

2

We got the cop, Shurm and I, and we went back. I wish I could skip this part. We went back and took the elevator to the second floor, and Shurm nearly fainted before we dragged him out. We got his keys and made him light the place up; I'd give a million if we hadn't insisted on that. Then we marched down the hall and into Room 11. At the door Shurm had another hysterical outburst, but we dragged him on in.

At first neither the cop nor I saw it. Shurm had us by the arms, screaming away.

"Before you look I want to tell you something. Remember when I said I recognized the voice that called Bailey's name? The voice belonged to the sixth head—the one I couldn't see so well—the one Bailey was afraid of. You know whose head it was, don't you?"

I guessed.

"It was Dr. Fiske's head," Shurm moaned. "Shawgi was his friend, and when Bailey double-crossed and killed him, Shawgi included him with the Indians in the revenge. Shawgi put Fiske's face on top of the totem pole; he put Fiske's soul there just as he did with the five dead Indians. Fiske called Bailey tonight!"

We pulled Shurm forward as we rounded the cases. And then we stood before the totem pole.

It was not easy to see the wooden pillar because there was a man standing against it—quite close against it, as though his arms were around it. A second glance, however, revealed the truth. *Its arms were around him!*

The wooden arms of the totem pole had closed about Bailey's body in a tight embrace. They had seized him as he stooped to fire the pole, and now they crushed him close—crushed him close against the five writhing heads, close against the pointed wooden teeth of the five mouths. And one mouth had his legs, another his thighs, a third his belly, a fourth his chest, a fifth his throat. The five pairs of mouths had bitten deep, and there was blood on wooden lips.

Bailey was staring upward with what was left of his face. It was simply a torn red mask that gazed into another mask—the sixth and uppermost face of the totem pole. The sixth face, as Shurm had said, was undoubtedly the face of a white man; the face of Dr. Fiske. And on the bloody lips rested not a smile, but a sardonic grin.